KAFKA IN LOVE

Kafka ᴵᴺ Love

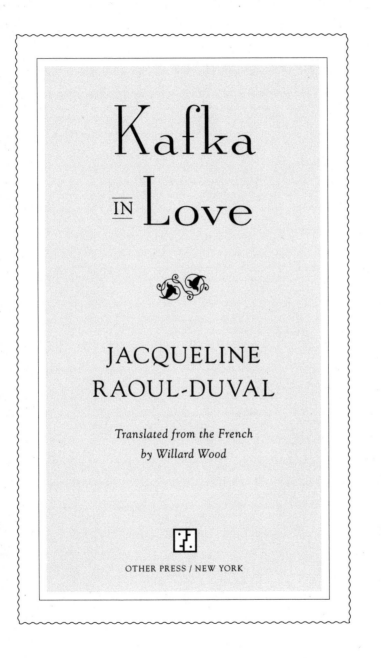

JACQUELINE RAOUL-DUVAL

*Translated from the French
by Willard Wood*

OTHER PRESS / NEW YORK

Production Editor: Yvonne E. Cárdenas
Text Designer: Jennifer Daddio/Bookmark Design & Media, Inc.
This book was set in 11.6 pt Goudy by
Alpha Design & Composition of Pittsfield, NH.

10 9 8 7 6 5 4 3 2 1

Library of Congress Cataloging-in-Publication Data

Raoul-Duval, Jacqueline.
[Kafka, l'eternel fiance. English]
Kafka in love / Jacqueline Raoul-Duval ; translated from
the French by Willard Wood.
p. cm.
ISBN 978-1-59051-541-9 (trade pbk. : acid-free paper) —
ISBN 978-1-59051-542-6 (eBook)   1. Kafka, Franz,
1883-1924—Fiction.   I. Wood, Willard.   II. Title.
PQ2678.A545K3413 2012
843'.914—dc23
2012012773

KAFKA IN LOVE

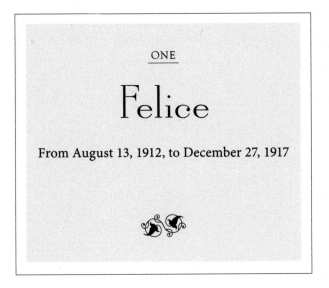

ONE

Felice

From August 13, 1912, to December 27, 1917

"I can love only what I can place so high above me that I cannot reach it."

"She is unattainable for me; I must resign myself to that, and my energies are in such a state that they do so jubilantly."

—LETTER TO MAX BROD

From the First Glance

O n this August 13, 1912, at the late hour when this story of singular loves begins, a south wind has swept away the banks of mist and the rain squalls that battered Prague all day. The stars are out, it is a true summer's night.

In the heart of the old city, on quiet Obstgasse Street, a young man in a light-colored suit, vestless and wearing a straw boater, walks hurriedly. In front of him, between the gaping paving stones, are puddles, glistening under the light of the streetlamps. Like a man in an obstacle race, he jumps from puddle to puddle, reflection to reflection, his feet neatly together. Here a decorated gable, there a window's arch, a church lintel, an apostle's outstretched arm, a pigeon taking flight. In accelerated time, he sees fragments of his city march past at his feet.

He is whistling "*Collection de boutons au Louvre*," which Leonie Frippon has been performing recently at the City of Vienna cabaret. Carrying a large red envelope under his arm, the young man is on his way—as on many nights—to visit his friend Max.

Max Brod and he met by chance at the university, on November 23, 1903. They were both working toward a doctorate in law, both with the same lack of enthusiasm. Max, already a leader, was at the center of a group of students, organizing conferences on literature and philosophy, his ruling passions. Giving a talk about Schopenhauer one evening, he called Nietzsche a charlatan. It sparked a debate, and he was applauded. As the hall emptied, a young man approached him. You cannot call Nietzsche a charlatan. In a few sentences, the stranger developed his thesis. A firm voice, a shy demeanor. Max examined the young righter of wrongs, who was taller than he by a head. He noticed the young man's elegance of dress, the tie and stand-up collar, the intensity of his gaze, his black eyes on fire. He was reminded of a Dostoyevsky hero.

The student's high-cheekboned thinness and distinction made Max uncomfortable, and he regretted having over-indulged in beer and fatty foods and neglected sports. But before Max could put his answer into words, the young man was gone. Where did this phantom come from? I've never seen him before, he has never participated in our meetings, never taken the floor. But can he have been reading the philosophers more attentively than all the rest of us?

The next morning, Max received a letter from the stranger. Along with apologies, it developed his argument. The reasoning was fine-grained, the style direct. Max kept this letter. And the dozens of others that followed. Several included little drawn figures, strange black marionettes hanging from invisible strings.

The two students became inseparable. They developed enthusiasms for the same books, the same movies, the cinematograph enthralled them. In late afternoon they could be seen leaving town together on long walks through the countryside. At night they attended the same shows, cheered and supported the Yiddish theater, patronized the same cafes. Max introduced his new friend to actors, young novelists, and poets, he knew all the most interesting literary circles, dance troupes, cabarets, and music halls in town.

Max confided to Franz that he wrote, but he was afraid to show him his writings. They were not up to his friend's literary standards. Standards that exasperated him even more than his friend's asceticism. Franz did not smoke, did not drink alcohol, coffee, or tea, slept by an open window even in the heart of winter, swam in icy rivers, and barely ate at all. Bad enough. But he would ruthlessly pluck a text naked, trim it of its fat: this metaphor made him despair of literature, that sentence was bombast, this other rang false, these two rubbed together like a tongue on a hollow tooth! He said once in a reverent voice, "You have to pull words from the void!"

"What void is that?" asked Max.

In answer, his friend extolled the pleasures of the commonplace, praised detail. "The smell of damp flagstones in a hall," he quoted, savoring each word, that is how one has to write.

On this August 13, 1912, at the late hour when this story of singular loves begins, the young man in the light-colored suit who was earlier chasing reflections of his ancient city rings at his friend's door.

"Do you know what time it is?" asks Max straightaway.

"He is always late," offers a voice from a nearby room.

"He sets his watch an hour and a half ahead, but he is still late with everyone! Strange, to set your watch forward an hour and a half!"

The young man laughs. He deposits his straw boater in the entry hall and proceeds into the dining room, which connects to a library and a small music room. Otto, Max's brother, is at the piano playing Lizst's Sonata in B Minor, their mother is on the telephone, Herr Brod is rummaging the shelves for a book. They wave a greeting at their evening visitor.

In the dining room, a young woman in a white blouse is eating dinner alone. Seeing her, the young man is for a moment undecided. Then he walks straight for her, stretches out his hand, and introduces himself.

"Franz Kafka."

He sits down across the table and looks so steadily at her that the young woman lowers her eyes and hesitates before answering.

"Felice Bauer."

"You're not from Prague. Where are you from? Are you traveling alone? How long will you spend here? What is your connection to the Brods? Do you work?"

Felice Bauer relaxes, answers in the same staccato: "I live in Berlin. I'm single. Related to the Brods by marriage. Yes, I work. I run the Parlograph department of the

Carl Lindström Company. And I leave tomorrow morning. Does that answer your questions?"

"I apologize, I'm always asking too many questions. May I keep you company?"

Without waiting for an answer, which wasn't coming, Franz Kafka draws a packet of photographs from his red envelope and empties the contents on the table.

"Fräulein, may I show you these photographs? Max and I took them in Weimar, where we spent several days together. Why are you eating all alone at this big table?"

"I came back late. I was at the theater. No one waited for me."

She smiles embarrassedly at Max, who comes to sit next to her. Franz shows her a photograph.

"Here is Goethe's house, first of all, with its fourteen windows on the street and—"

"You counted them?" says Max.

"I am envious of everything that touches Goethe, absolutely everything. His parlor. His study. The staircase made by a convict from a giant oak tree, without a single nail. His Chinese porcelains. His bust, sculpted by David d'Angers. His garden theater with its two rows of seats for spectators. And even the gold laurel wreath over his casket, given by the German women of Prague."

He picks out other photographs.

"We bribed the watchman, and he let us take pictures of everything, even the bedroom with its canopy bed. Would you like to see?"

Felice looks at each snapshot attentively. She pushes her unfinished plate away.

"Your meat is getting cold," says Max.

"There is nothing more revolting than people who can't stop eating," says Felice.

A serving girl comes in to tell Herr Brod, who is reading in the library, that he is wanted on the telephone.

He rises and leaves the room.

"There is nothing more revolting than the telephone ringing," says Max.

Felice describes the first scene of the operetta she has just seen at the Residenz Theater, *The Auto Sweetheart.*

"The telephone rings fifteen times in a row. Somebody, using the same patter, calls each of the fifteen characters on the stage to the phone, one after another."

"Luckily, we aren't so many," says Max.

Felice continues looking through the photographs, while Franz offers a running commentary.

"Here is Liszt's house. He only worked, apparently, from five to eight in the morning. Then he went to church, then back to bed, and at eleven he received visitors. This photograph shows Schiller's house. The waiting room, the parlor, the study, the sleeping alcoves. Well laid out for a writer's house."

Max snatches a picture that Franz was trying to hide.

"Look at this one of Franz swimming. Traveling with him is pure hell. At every town, often after hours of wandering, we would have to find a hotel with no other guests, no dogs nearby, absolute quiet, and within easy distance of a vegetarian restaurant and an outdoor swimming pool. If he doesn't swim, row, or walk every day, he becomes impossible."

"Do you often travel together?"

"Yes. We've been to Italy together, Brescia, to see the airplanes, Milan, Riva, Lugano, Zurich. And twice to Paris. Otto was with us. He helped me deal with the demands of our nudist."

"You're a nudist?"

"Not really . . . I'm the man in the bathing suit. It is true that this summer, at the Jungborn colony, it made me a little sick to see people all naked and unconcerned. When they run, it doesn't help things. And I'm not crazy about old men jumping over haystacks."

They all three laugh.

"So why do you go there?"

"The people are quiet, they live close to nature. You sleep under the open sky, walk barefoot through the grass in the early morning. It's very pleasant."

Max holds up another photograph for Felice.

"Look at Franz in front of Werther's garden with Grete. They're eating cherries."

"Who is Grete?"

"The caretaker's lovely daughter. Franz followed her day and night. Admit it, you were in love with her. You gave her chocolates, bunches of carnations, a little heart with a chain, who knows what else? You'd have asked her to marry you if she'd responded."

Max looks at his watch.

"It's already eleven o'clock and we haven't decided on the sequence for your stories. You have to send them off first thing in the morning. Let's sit in the next room while Felice finishes dinner."

He rises, picks up the red envelope from the table in front of Franz, and pulls out a manuscript. Felice looks at Franz in surprise.

"Are you a writer too?"

Max answers in his place: "Especially Franz! Writing is his reason for being. His head is crammed with unbelievable stories. He goes crazy if he doesn't write them down. He is made of literature. You've never read anything by him?"

Felice pages through the tome of Goethe left by Herr Brod on his armchair.

"No, but I've read all your books, Max. Except for your first novel, *Nornepygge Castle*. I couldn't get through it. I tried several times."

Franz looks at her, appalled. There is a silence, which Felice breaks in a calm voice.

"I'm more surprised than anybody. I intend to pick it up again when I have the chance."

Max leads Franz to a pedestal table with three stiff, slender feet.

"Let's get to work. It will only take us a few minutes. I have a proposal for you, which I've written down somewhere. Where did I put it?"

He searches through his pockets, looks all around him, and finally notices it on the mantelpiece.

"There it is! I've put 'Children on the Road' first, followed by 'The Excursion into the Mountains' and 'Desire to Be a Red Indian.' For the last story, I've chosen 'Being Unhappy.' As far as all the others, I agree with the order you suggested."

Felice approaches them.

"I love to transcribe manuscripts. I do it in Berlin occasionally. I'd be very grateful, Max, if you would send me some."

Franz looks at her. "To read the text, or just to transcribe it?"

"Just to transcribe it."

Franz smacks his hand down on the pedestal table. All three jump.

"Franz, do you agree with the sequence I proposed? Can I put your stories away?"

"I won't mail out anything tomorrow."

"You're not starting that again! Every time you get a chance to publish I have to fight with you. Why this last-minute refusal?"

"Because there's no reason to publish a text that isn't perfect. I'm in no hurry. Man was expelled from paradise because of his impatience. And it's his impatience that keeps him from returning. Anyway, I don't want to disappoint your editor again."

"But he's the one who keeps asking me for your text. He called on the telephone again yesterday! I gave him my solemn word that you would mail the manuscript to him tomorrow morning. You can't do this to me."

"I asked him how many copies of my first collection he had sold. Eleven. As I'd bought ten of them, I want to know who owns the eleventh *Meditation*. And why does your editor publish texts that don't sell?"

"Because he knows that one day he'll sell hundreds

of them. Do you want me to remind you of all the things that Rilke, Werfel, and Musil have said about you? You're not leaving here until you promise to send out the text tomorrow."

"At the central post office, go to the young woman at window 14, she's the prettiest," Otto interjects.

"Send it as a registered letter," says Max.

"I have never sent a letter, or even a postcard, except as registered mail."

Otto has closed the piano lid. He kneels in front of the wood stove. Franz looks at him and laughs, saying to Felice: "Otto likes to go to bed early. Every time I visit, he makes a great show of fussing with the fire screen. It's his way of reminding me that it's time to go. He calls me the professional disturber of sleep. Sometimes it takes the combined forces of the whole Brod family to shoo me from the apartment. I'm afraid that tonight I've kept you up late too. What time do you leave tomorrow morning?"

"Six-thirty. I haven't packed my bag yet. And I want to finish my book before closing my eyes."

Franz smiles. "Do you like staying up late with a book?"

"Sometimes until dawn."

"Are you returning to Berlin?"

"No, I'm off to Budapest. To attend my sister's wedding. Do you really want to know everything?"

Frau Brod joins the conversation: "At her hotel, Felice showed me the batiste gown she plans to wear at the ceremony. Lovely!"

Felice stands up. Franz, not taking his eyes off her, says, "Are you really wearing Frau Brod's slippers?"

"Yes. The weather was terrible all day, and my boots needed drying. But I'm used to wearing high-heeled mules."

"High-heeled mules! What a novelty!"

She flies off down the hallway leading to the bathroom. A door slams. Frau Brod says, "Felice is such a gazelle!"

Franz makes a face. Max sidles over to him and asks quietly, "How do you like our Berliner?"

"No charm, no appeal. When I arrived, she was having dinner at the dining room table, but I took her for the maid. Her face is bony, empty. Her nose almost seems broken, her hair is blond, quite straight. She is dressed like a housewife, although she isn't one at all, as I quickly realized. She is decisive, self-confident, strong. As might . . ."

Steps sound in the hallway. He stops in midsentence, hurries to intercept Felice, pulling a magazine from his envelope to show her: "Fräulein Felice, I happen to have brought an issue of *Palästina*."

Felice holds out a hand and Franz takes it, pressing it to him.

"Do you know this magazine? Max and I plan to go to Palestine next year. Would you like to join us?"

"What a strange idea . . . Are you joking?"

She frees her hand.

"Not in the slightest, I've never been more serious."

"It's not a trip that you decide on at the drop of a hat! Do you speak Hebrew?"

"No, not really. But my great-grandfather on my mother's side, who gave me my Hebrew name, Amschel, was a famous Talmud scholar, and I'm studying modern Hebrew. Will you come? I'd like it if you made a promise. A formal promise."

"I don't know. Let me think about it. And bid my hosts good night."

Having followed her into the hallway, Franz watches as Felice puts on a wide-brimmed beige-and-white hat, which she anchors in place with three long pins. Herr Brod offers to accompany her back to the hotel.

"May I join you?" asks Franz.

In the narrow street with its uneven cobbles, Herr Brod and Felice walk side by side. Franz follows them, strangely tongue-tied. Halfway to the hotel, he wonders if he might be able to bring this young woman flowers at the station. But where is he to find flowers at the crack of dawn? Gripped by anxiety, desire, and confusion, he trips on the sidewalk several times for no reason and steps out into the street. As they start down Perlgasse, Felice turns to him.

"Where do you live?"

"You want my address?"

He feels a burst of joy, she is going to write him, agree to join his trip to Palestine.

"Your address? No, I'd like to make sure that I'm not taking you too far out of your way in going to my hotel. And keeping you up too late."

"I'm never in a hurry to go home. I sleep very little. My nights consist of two parts: one wakeful, the other sleepless."

Felice resumes her conversation with Herr Brod. Franz hears them wasting time comparing the traffic in Prague to the traffic in Berlin. Herr Brod then offers the young woman travel advice, naming several train stations where she can find a bite to eat. Felice announces that she plans to have breakfast in the dining car. She is hoping to find her umbrella, which she left in the train several days before.

They enter the lobby of a luxury hotel, The Blue Star. Franz is so absorbed that he slips into the same compartment of the revolving door as Felice and steps all over her feet. He babbles his apology. They say good-bye in front of the open door of the elevator. Franz reminds her of their travel plans. Felice catches sight of the doorman and arranges for a car to bring her to the station in the morning. They make their good-byes a second time. Felice says, "You are going to remind me again . . ."

Franz interrupts her. "No, no, I have just one last question: How long can you keep chocolate before it goes bad?"

A Passion Without Love

On September 20, 1912, he writes his first letter to Felice Bauer. On letterhead of the Workers' Accident Insurance Institute, where he holds an important post. A letter that is two pages long, typed on a typewriter he is unfamiliar with, and started after his sixth hour at the office. He reminds her of his name, Franz Kafka, their meeting at the Brods', and their plan to travel to Palestine together. In case she sees no reason to accept him as her traveling companion and as a guide, burden, tyrant, or whatever else he might become, he suggests that in the meantime she accept him provisionally as her correspondent. He adds that he is not punctual and that, in exchange, he does not expect to receive regular letters.

He signs: "Yours very sincerely, Dr. Franz Kafka." (He is a doctor of law.)

This first letter remains unanswered.

Franz writes a second one, in longhand. He has much to say: it is a warm, sunny day, the window is open, he is humming a tune. He explains to Felice Bauer that for five weeks he begged high and low for her office address in Berlin, that anxieties rain down on him continuously, that he composed his first letter over the course of ten nights, so difficult did he find transcribing what he had in his head before going to sleep. He signs the letter: "Yours, Franz Kafka."

Felice does not answer these five handwritten pages. But she keeps both letters.

Determined to break through the silence erected by the young woman against him, Franz seeks the help of his friends. Both Max and his sister, Sophie Friedmann, who is married to a cousin of the Bauers, write to Felice to vaunt their friend's merits and suggest the high consideration in which he is held. After three weeks and a second letter from Sophie, Felice finally relents. Franz is elated. Her letter, he says, makes him feel absurdly happy, and he puts his hand on it to feel that it really belongs to him.

He then embarks on a frenetic correspondence. From October 23, when he receives her first reply, to December 31, he sends Felice one hundred letters, often two or three a day.

The first ones are delicious: "I tremble like a lunatic when I receive your letters, my heart beats through my entire body and is conscious only of you."

"Dear Fräulein Felice, it is one-thirty in the morning. There is hardly a quarter of an hour of my waking day when I don't think of you, and many when I do nothing else. Since the evening when we met, I've felt as though I have a hole in my chest through which everything flows into me and is sucked out of me. You are intimately associated with my writing."

"Today I received your last three letters almost at once. Your goodness is infinite. I shall most likely write you several more times again today. Farewell, then, but only for a few hours."

The tone grows progressively less ceremonious. The "Dear Fräulein Bauer" of the early letters gives way to "Dear Fräulein Felice," then to "Dearest Fräulein Felice." Suddenly, on November 14, he writes, "Dearest, dearest," and boldly shifts to the familiar *Du*. A few days later he writes, "Dearest, very dearest! Most cherished of my temptations, my beloved, to answer your question: yes,

I fell in love with you at once, that night at Max's, right from the start, from the first glance. I love you so much it makes me groan."

"Dearest, very dearest! I dreamed about you again. A mailman was bringing me your two letters, one in each hand, his arms moving in precision, like the jerking of piston rods in a steam engine. I kept pulling page after page from the envelopes but they never emptied. It was a magical dream!" He signs the letter: "Your Franz."

From the first and over the course of months, he paints the young woman a portrait of himself: faithful, pitiless, ludicrous, funny, and, as he says explicitly, untruthful.

"You take me for much younger than I am, I almost feel like hiding my age. I will be 30 on July 3. I do look like a boy, though."

In his *Diaries*, he engages in more detailed scrutiny, having looked at himself attentively in the mirror. "My face appeared to me better than I know it to be. True, it was dusk and the light was coming from behind me, so that only the down on the rims of my ears was lit. A pure face, nicely shaped, its contour almost beautiful. The black hair, eyebrows, and eye sockets jump out livingly from the dormant mass of the face. The eyes are not ravaged, there is no trace of that, but neither are they childlike, rather unbelievably energetic, but perhaps only because they were observing, since I was just then observing myself and trying to frighten myself."

He tells Felice that he is the thinnest man in the world, but that he is no longer ashamed of his body since he started going to the swimming pool.

And he answers each of her questions: "Would you like to know my timetable? Very regular. From 8 to 2 at the office, lunch until 3 or 3:30, then a nap in bed until 7:30, followed by ten minutes of exercises, naked at the open window, then an hour's walk, alone or with a friend, then dinner with all of my family. Then at 10:30 (sometimes later) I start to write. This continues, depending on my strength, desire, and luck, until 1, 2, or 3 in the morning."

He appends to the letter (by way of warning?) a poem by Yüan Tzu-tsai:

A cold night, absorbed in my book,
I have forgotten bedtime. The fragrances
Sprinkled on my gold-embroidered bedcover
Have dissipated, the fire has gone out.
My lover, who has contained her wrath
Until now, snatches the lamp from me:
"Do you know what time it is?"

He makes no secret of his oddness: "My mode of life? It would seem crazy and unbearable to you. I dress any old way. The same suit does for the office, the street, and my desk at home, summer and winter. I am more hardened to the cold than a tree stump and have not yet worn an overcoat this year, light or heavy, though it is now mid-November. Among pedestrians muffled up in their warm clothes, I look like a lunatic in my little summer hat and summer suit without a vest (I am the inventor of the suit without a vest)."

"Needless to say, I don't smoke and I don't drink alcohol, coffee, or tea." But, perhaps as a reassurance to Felice, he adds that when people around him are drinking black coffee or beer it makes him feel happy. Nothing gives him more pleasure than to see others eating something he would never put in his mouth.

Wanting to give the full picture, he continues: "I eat three meals a day, but nothing between meals, literally nothing. In the morning stewed fruit, biscuits, and milk. At 2:30, out of filial pity, the same as the others, a bit less than the others. Winter evenings at 9:30: yogurt, whole-grain bread, butter, walnuts and hazelnuts, chestnuts, dates, figs, raisins, almonds, pumpkin seeds, bananas, apples, pears, oranges. And I never get my fill of lemonade.

But dearest Felice, please don't reject me because of this, accept me kindly."

In his *Diaries*, he lets loose and confesses his hankerings, real and imaginary: "This craving that I almost always have, if ever I feel my stomach empty, to heap up in me images of terrible feats of eating. I especially satisfy this craving in front of pork butchers. If I see a sausage labeled as an old, hard farmhouse sausage, I bite into it in my imagination with my teeth and swallow quickly, regularly, and mechanically. The despair that always follows this act, imaginary though it is, increases my haste. I shove long slabs of ribs into my mouth unchewed, then bring them out again the other end, pulling them through my stomach and intestines. I empty whole grocery stores, filthy ones, cram myself with herrings, pickles, and all the spicy, gamey, unhealthy foods. Hard candies pour into my mouth like hail from their cast-iron pots."

He gives a minute description of his daily life, his outings, his idleness, his obsessions, and his weaknesses.

"The bathroom," he tells Felice, "gives me much pleasure. I was so bored last night that I went to the bathroom to wash my hands three times in succession. And I sometimes spend a whole afternoon with my hair. And with my brush, made by an English firm, G. B. Kent & Sons. I'm quite taken with it."[1]

He reproaches himself for being too fond of creature comforts. When the housemaid forgets to bring him hot water in the morning it disturbs him profoundly. He has long been obsessed with his comfort and ensures it by begging, crying, and forgoing more important things.

To his young lady in Berlin, to Max, to his friends, to his parents, Franz complains year after year about the noise around him: "My room is the headquarters of all the commotion in the apartment. I hear the doors slam. My sister Valli shouts through the hallway as though it were a Paris street to ask whether Father's hat has been brushed. There is loud talking in the rooms on either side, women's voices to the left, men's voices to the right. I have the impression that the people are wild beings, blabbering with no sense of meaning, speaking only to disturb the air and watch their words float past. The large room is full of clamor, the sound of a card game and, later, of Father's normal conversation, conducted without much coherence but in resonant tones."

---

1 This hairbrush, the only personal possession of Kafka's still in existence, is in Israel at the Kibbutz En Sharod, the gift of Dora, his fourth fiancée.

The automobiles in the street make a terrible noise. A monstrous ruckus. Franz is forced to stuff his ears with wax. "It's awful to plug one's ears during one's lifetime!"

He provides a quick sketch of his family. He has three sisters: Elli, the oldest, who is married; Valli, the middle one, who has just become engaged; and Ottla, the youngest, who is his favorite. She is pure, true, and honest, with a perfect balance of humility and pride, devotion and independence, shyness and courage.

His mother spends all her time in the store helping her husband. Franz sees little of her and only at night, when she returns exhausted after an endless day of work. "My mother," says Franz, "is the loving slave of my father, a giant, and my father is the loving tyrant of my mother. The harmony between them is perfect."

Speaking of his mother, he realizes that he has not always loved her as she deserves, because the German language has prevented him from doing so. "The Jewish mother is not a *Mutter*," he writes. "To call her *Mutter* makes her foreign and a little comical. *Mutter* is peculiarly German, it contains Christian splendor, but also Christian coldness."

One night he announces to Felice that his oldest sister has just had her first child. His mother returned at one a.m. with the news that a baby boy had been born. His father marched through the apartment in his nightshirt throwing open all the doors, waking his son, his daughters, even the maid, and proclaiming the child's birth as though the child had not simply come into the world but already lived a life full of honor and been buried with great pomp. "I didn't feel the least affection for this nephew, only envy, a fierce envy," says Franz, "because I will never have children."

Was Felice troubled by this warning?

In each of his letters, Franz bombards Felice with questions: What time do you arrive at the office? What do you eat for breakfast? What do you see from your office window? What are you wearing? Give me the names of your male and female friends, tell me what the weather is like, what show did you go see? Did you have dinner before or after the theater? Where did you sit? How do you spend your Sundays, what books are you reading? What is this tango that you are dancing, is it an import from Mexico? How can you dictate something to two girls at once? What colleague did you run back to the house with on the thirtieth? Why did you not go for a walk all day?

My head, he says, is as full of questions as a field is of flies.

Insatiably, as though drawing nourishment from her, he extorts the promise to write him every day. "Write me a new letter right away. Answer all my questions exactly, I want answers as sharp and quick as snakes. Good-bye, and remember to keep a little diary. I am obliged to write you, or I would die of sadness."

He echoes this thought in his *Diaries*: "To have beside one a person who would have this understanding, a wife perhaps, would mean to have support on all sides, to have God."

By the early part of November, when they have been corresponding barely two months, a lament arises and grows louder and louder: What have I done that you torment me in this way? Today again nothing, neither in the first mail nor the second. How you make me suffer! When just a word from you would make me happy. Just two lines, a greeting, an envelope, a card, I beg you! Since Friday I have sent you 14 or 15 letters. Madness.

When his suffering becomes unbearable, he sends her an urgent telegram, and the handful of words he gets in return restore his calm for a few hours. He uses the telephone only rarely, his heart pounding as he waits for the connection, but he finds it distracting to speak in front of others at the office, he stammers, he can't hear a thing.

"You'd do better to stop staring at the earpiece and put your ear to it," said one of his colleagues mockingly. Franz hung up the telephone and fled, as though he'd been caught doing something wrong.

Before long he is begging Felice to put a stop to their exchange of letters, he cannot stand the torment: "If I want to go on living, I cannot continue vainly waiting for news of you. Don't write me anymore."

When a letter arrives for him the next day, he is seized with remorse and begs Felice to forgive his harassment: "May I kiss you? On this deplorable paper? I might as well open the window and kiss the night air. You will write again, won't you?"

He sends her innocent roses, to clear the air of his criminal words.

Then he asks her to write him only once a week, on Saturday, as he cannot bear to receive her daily letters. Three days later, he is begging her repeatedly to write him every day.

They exchange photographs. The first one that Felice receives makes her burst out laughing: Franz is only five years old, dressed as a girl, and glaring at her. A few days later, he sends her a photograph of two naked babies: his sisters. He is hoping that Felice will send him a picture of herself at that age, but in vain. Finally he sends her a picture of himself in front of his house: a young dandy in a necktie, wearing an open, dark overcoat, a gray suit, and a homburg that casts a shadow over his face. His eyes are hidden. Yet Felice cannot tear her own eyes away from his gaze. The narrow pants, perfectly creased, emphasize the thinness of his legs. His round-toed shoes, which are solid and new, gleam. His hands are crossed over his stomach. Felice puts the portrait in a frame on her night table. It watches over her at night as she falls asleep.

He for his part becomes rapt contemplating photographs of his Felice and constantly asks her to send more: "A face," he says, "can be grasped only through a thousand photographs." He also wants pictures of her sisters, her aunt, her niece, and her friends. As soon as they reach him, he fires off questions to her: Where were the photographs taken, by whom, at what time of day, and what is around them, beyond the frame? The unseen surroundings interest him more than what is visible. "The photographs are beautiful and necessary, but they are also a torment. You can never provide me with enough explanations."

After their first meetings, Franz stops asking her for pictures. He has looked at her too long in the flesh for photographs to be of any use. He no longer wants to look at them: Felice appears flat and commonplace. "I have gazed," he explains, "into your real, your human face with its inevitable faults and lost myself in it. How can I emerge and find my way around mere photographs?"

He complains about the office, that pit of pain, that tedious paper mill tearing at his flesh. He complains about the asbestos factory his father bought with his son-in-law but wants his son to manage instead of writing inanities. He complains about everything that keeps him from writing. "My life consists and has always consisted of attempts to write, usually unsuccessful. But when I don't write, I am on the floor and fit only to be swept up." He adds this statement, the first of many of its kind: "My strength being very limited, I was forced to give up a little bit on every side, so that I would have just enough energy for what strikes me as my main goal. My nights can never be long enough for the business of writing, which, incidentally, is highly voluptuous."

When he meets Felice in August, he has been lazing around for months and has done nothing but sprawl on his couch. He has even been neglecting his *Diaries*, barely writing an occasional sentence: "My left hand embraced the fingers of my right hand out of pity. I was on bad terms with myself because I had gone too long without writing."

Then on the night of September 22–23, two days after he sends his first letter to Berlin, the wave sweeps in again and lifts him up. He writes "The Judgment" in a single sitting from ten at night to six in the morning. When he puts his pen down, the sky is just starting to lighten. He is so happy that he takes the time to write down his impressions in his *Diaries* at length: "I advanced parting the waters in front of me. Only in this way can writing be done, only with this continuity, with this complete opening of the body and the soul. Everything can be expressed, even the strangest ideas."

As he is stretching afterward, the maid, Ruzenka, crosses the entrance hall, her eyes swollen with sleep. He calls on her to witness the moment: "I've been writing all night!"

Then, like an athlete taking a victory lap around the stadium, he turns off his lamp and goes hammering on the doors of his sisters.

This story, "The Judgment," makes tears come to his eyes when, on the following day, he reads it to his friends at Oskar Baum's house.[2] Until the day of his death, he

---

2 Oskar Baum, who was blinded as a schoolboy, was nonetheless an excellent pianist, poet, and writer. He died in Prague in 1941 during the Occupation.

continued to believe this story, which he owed to Felice, could "stand," whereas so much else of what he wrote he ordered to be burnt.

The text is dedicated to Fräulein Felice B., to the young lady he saw one night for barely an hour.

Berlin, Seven Months Later

From September 1912 to March 1913, Franz and Felice write letters back and forth without interruption and without major developments. Except for one critical thing: Franz keeps writing at the same feverish pitch. He pushes out "The Metamorphosis" in a period of twenty days (from November 17 to December 7) "like an actual delivery, covered in filth and mucus." The paternity of this story, which Elias Canetti called one of the major masterpieces of the twentieth century, Franz attributes to Felice.

He writes after nightfall. He waits for his parents, whose apartment he lives in, to finish their noisy card parties and for the household to fall asleep. He shuts himself in his room, which he describes in his *Diaries* inch by inch as though filming it. A small room, narrow, with a sofa, and a bed covered in a red quilt. His desk is littered with a thousand objects, a shaving mirror, a clothes brush, an open coin purse, a solitary key, a necktie half wrapped around a detachable collar, pencils, an empty matchbox, a paperweight, a ruler, many collar studs, some razor blades, and several tie clips. From the open drawer spill brochures, old newspapers, catalogs, postcards, and half-torn letters.

On his walls he has hung two works of art that he sees whenever he raises his head: a print of *The Plowman* by the painter Hans Thoma, and a cast of a headless maenad, her body draped in flowing robes and brandishing a leg of beef.

When his own legs grow numb, Franz gets up from his desk and stands at the window looking out on the street. His head back, his cheek pressed against the window catch, he watches the river stream by in front of him, the banks where the grass is starting to turn yellow or turn green, the sky starting to change colors, and the cars parading past, drawing him back into the world of men.

Franz is an insatiable reader and lives surrounded by books. We know just how much he valued his library: one night when he was out, his mother entered his room and took a novel by Oskar Baum that Franz had intended to lend his sister Elli. When Franz found out, he flew into an absolute rage, almost swearing at his mother: "Leave me my books! I have nothing else."

He reads biographies, memoirs, novels, essays, and poetry collections, rereading the works he particularly admires two or three times or more. He asks Felice what she is reading, deplores her choices, and recommends that she read Flaubert (he dreams of reading *Sentimental Education*[3] out loud to an audience in a single sitting, taking as many days and nights as necessary, in French of course), Dostoyevsky, Strindberg, Grillparzer, Kropotkin, Gogol, Kleist, Dickens, Jammes, Berlioz's autobiography . . . the list is endless. "We should read only books that bite and sting, a book must be the ax for the frozen sea inside us."

He writes down an anecdote he can't bring himself to tell Felice: it is unlawful to think of the Torah in the bathroom, and for that reason you can read profane books there. A certain K. had a great deal of profane knowledge, he had learned everything he knew in the bathroom. No detail is trivial, Franz adds, as long as it is accurate.

---

3 Kafka never went on a trip without slipping this book into his luggage.

On December 11, 1912, he sends Felice *Meditation*, which has just been published. He waits feverishly for her comments, avidly reading the letters he receives from her almost every morning. Nothing, not a word about the book. Days go by. Still nothing. On December 18 he injects a slight nudge: "I am so happy to think that my book is in your possession." He waits. Still nothing. Felice prattles on about everything except his book. She is not interested in what is best in me, he thinks. Her indifference humiliates him, tortures him. On December 23 he brings the issue into the open: "You have not said anything yet about my book."

Felice says nothing, she has not had the curiosity to open it, though she reads voraciously and waxes enthusiastic about dozens of books. Franz finds the names of so many writers in her letters that he is jealous and would like to pick a quarrel with them, all of them. One day she praises Schnitzler to the skies, and Franz is furious. He writes her in the middle of the night. His tone is icy: "I don't like him at all and don't hold him in respect. He can never drop low enough in the public's opinion."

On Sunday, December 29, he explodes: "Why don't you tell me in two words that you don't like my little book? It would be understandable that you don't know what to make of it, and I might still hope that it would some day appeal to you. A hesitant opinion on your part would seem quite natural to me, but you have said nothing. Twice you announced something, but then said nothing. You don't like my book as such, but since I wrote it you must like it all the same—in which case a person gets around to reading it."

He spends that Sunday in misery.

After this humiliating exchange, Franz no longer speaks of his work to Felice, or says very little. Before, he would give her a full daily account, detailed, enthusiastic, and funny. He had hoped for praise, a little admiration. He receives nothing but stinging silence.

He writes her every day but makes no plans to see her. Instead, he voices vague regrets: "You flew into the elevator, the night we met, instead of whispering in my ear despite the presence of Herr Brod: 'Come with me to Berlin, leave everything and come.'" At times he accuses himself of inertia: "Why, fool that I am, did I stay at the office or at home, instead of jumping on the train with my eyes shut, to open them only when I am near you?"

Most likely prompted by Felice, he hints at the beginning of December that he might visit Berlin at Christmastime. However, nothing is less certain. The trip starts to seem even more doubtful. "But," he pleads, "you too,

Felice, will have relatives visiting who might bar me from Berlin."

In January there is no longer any question of seeing each other. On February 5 he is evasive: "At Easter, would you have an hour free for me on Sunday or on Monday and, if so, do you think it would be a good idea for me to come?"

Two days later he writes: "Dearest, I don't want to see your relatives, I am not strong enough for that. So think about it carefully, Felice. Your parents, your father, your brother, and your sister from Dresden will surely be at home, and I can therefore easily imagine that you wouldn't have the time."

Do these seem like the words of a lover? Or a thinly disguised attempt to avoid a meeting that he does not look forward to? He confesses: "You are right, Felice, I have often had to force myself to write you in the last few days."

The reason for this change?

"My American novel.[4] The story I am writing takes place entirely in the United States of America. It is my

---

4 Kafka drew details of daily life in America from Benjamin Franklin's *Autobiography*, which he read with great enjoyment and recommended to his father.

first somewhat longer work after fifteen years of frustrated effort. It must be completed, and so, with your blessing I plan to spend the brief moments I might otherwise employ writing inaccurate, alarmingly incomplete, imprudent, dangerous letters to you, on this task where everything has grown calm and is headed along the right path. But don't abandon me, Felice, to my terrible loneliness."

In choosing between Berlin and New York, between the pleasure of seeing the woman he loves and bringing a character into the world, naming him ("Karl Rossmann"), giving him a life in a bustling city on the other side of the planet (to which he knows he will never go), Franz does not hesitate for a second. Felice has supplied him the strength, the exaltation that he needs. She produced the spark, and the motor has caught and started to run. She performed magnificently the task that he set for her on the night they met. He loves her all the more for it. Or rather, he needs the passion that he feels for her.

A passion without love.

Exhilarated by his writing, he jokes: "Dearest, I beg you with my hands raised in supplication not to be jealous. If the people in my novel notice your jealousy, they will abandon me. And consider a bit that if they leave me, I will be obliged to follow them, even if it means going all the way to hell, where they are at home. No, I will not sever myself from my novel even when you are here. Surely not."

A few days later he crows: "Cry, dearest, cry, the time to cry has come! The hero of my little story has just died. It may comfort you to know that he died quite peacefully and reconciled to all."

Then in March, Franz collapses. He is working too much. The office, the asbestos factory, his reading, his correspondence with Felice, Max, Oskar Baum, Felix Weltsch, Ernst Weiss, and his sisters leave him no peace, his insomnia is worsening, his health is failing. His novel is stalled.

He confesses his crushing doubts to Max. But his old friend has married Elsa, and a married friend is no longer a true friend. Franz misses seeing Max every night, going on trips with him.

On January 12, his second sister, Valli, also marries. He feels more and more alone. A man without a wife is not a human being, the Talmud's imprecation haunts him.

Felice is his only port in the storm. If he wants to stay attached to her, he has to do more than write, he cannot go on avoiding her. In March the trip to Berlin becomes a necessity.

Franz's first visit to Berlin, more than seven months after their original meeting, can be told in a few words. A lightning visit, announced as problematic, which Franz cancels and then reinstates as a possibility: "Still undecided." And which he then confirms on Friday night by express letter.

On Saturday, March 22, 1913, he leaps into the train with his eyes closed. When he opens them again in Berlin, it is 10:30 at night and Felice is not on the platform. Reeling with fatigue, for as usual he has traveled third class, Franz goes to the Hotel Askanischer Hof. No word of welcome awaits him there. Anxious at the thought of actually seeing the woman he has been writing for seven months, he is unable to sleep.

The next morning at 8:30, he sends her a note: "What has happened, Felice? Here I am in Berlin, but I will have to leave again this afternoon at 4 or 5. The hours are passing, and I hear nothing from you. Please send me an answer back with the boy." The bicycle messenger returns with the words: "I will telephone you in a quarter of an hour."

By the time they meet, strained and excited, it is almost eleven o'clock. He gives her a hug and a furtive kiss on the cheek. They walk in the Tiergarten, it is chilly, the trees have hardly opened their buds. Felice has a funeral to attend at noon. She doesn't want to be late, they run like lunatics, it's the best moment of their meeting, they laugh, their movements are unhampered, they hold hands. At the cemetery, they part company. Franz watches the young lady walk off between two strange men as the procession gets under way. He doesn't consider following her, staying at her side. They have agreed to talk by telephone at three o'clock, and Felice has made a promise: she will accompany Franz to the station. He has lunch, visits his good friend, the surgeon and writer Ernst Weiss, and returns to the hotel well before three. There he waits. From the lobby, he looks out at a cold, persistent rain that will continue falling until dusk. He considers going out to buy a newspaper, the *Berliner Tagenblatt*, but he is afraid to come across a news item that would upset him. He has not yet forgotten the report of a recent trial: a certain Marie Abraham, twenty-three, driven by hunger and poverty, strangled her daughter Barbara, nine months old, with the man's necktie that she used as a garter. The image of this young mother breaking her baby's neck haunts him. Though Franz prides himself on never crying, he sobbed over this news brief.

He could go to a cafe and read or write. But no, he stays in his chair by the telephone, like a soldier in his sentry box.

Berlin is a city that Franz knows. He would like to live there if he could ever get away from Prague and the clutches of his family. In 1910 he saw a production of *Ham-let* with Bassermann in the title role. In his mind he sees him again, alone on the stage. He tries to imagine why an actor of such great talent would accept a role in *The Other One*, a very mediocre film that he saw with Max.

Perhaps he nods off in his chair, perhaps Karl Ross-mann comes and sits beside him, perhaps he flits around himself like a bird chased from its nest.

At four o'clock he runs to the station, walks the length of the platform in both directions. The train starts, Felice has not come. The rain that is still pattering down might have prevented her, he tells himself, but no one could have stopped her from calling me on the telephone.

He has traveled sixteen hours to catch a glimpse of her. And he didn't bring himself to say what he had to say. Several times he has hinted at it in his letters, but to no effect. Felice has not wanted to understand or even to sus-pect. Face to face with her, he said nothing.

Once back in Prague, he dithers for several days, un-able to come out with his "great confession." On April 1, he finds the strength to write. The letter starts abruptly, without any form of address, as though he were not speaking to Felice but to himself, as though he needed to cough up the words that were choking him: "My real fear—nothing worse could be said or heard—is that I will never be able to possess you. At best, like an endlessly faithful dog, I would go only so far as to kiss your limply surrendered hand, which will not be an act of love, but a sign of the despair felt by an animal condemned to silence and eternal separation. I would feel the breath and life of your body at my side, yet be further from you than I am now, here in this room. I would be excluded from you forever."

He signs, then rereads, what he believes to be his death sentence.

He is preparing for bed and starting to get undressed when his mother gives a little knock on the door: "May I come in?"

He smiles at her. "You aren't bothering me."

This late and unaccustomed visit seems to offer a plot development.

"Have you written your Uncle Alfred?"

Franz reassures his mother: "I mailed my letter to him yesterday."

Emboldened by his thoughtfulness, she goes to him and plants a good-night kiss on his cheek, which she hasn't done for years.

"That's good," says Franz, and pats his mother's hand.

"I never dared," says his mother. "I thought you didn't like it. But if you do like it, I like it very much, too."

Touched, she slips out the door. Once alone, Franz sits again at his desk, pulls the letter from its envelope, and adds a postscript. He tells Felice about his mother's unexpected visit, the words they exchanged, her kiss. Setting down a fragment of life has the effect of changing his mood, restoring his freedom as a writer.

The next day, proud of his courage, he writes to Max: "Yesterday, I sent my great confession to Berlin. She is truly a martyr!"

And Felice's reaction? "You are drifting away from me, at a time when you are critically necessary to me."

"I am critically necessary to you?"

Franz is elated, he has no cause for fear, he did not receive the answer that his letter deserved. He sighs with relief: "I, dearest, drift away? I, who breathe only through you? I look for you everywhere. In the street, the gestures of all sorts of people remind me of you. I, drift away, I who die of longing for you?"

He confesses that when he was washing his hands in the dark passage that very morning, he felt such a strong desire from thinking about her that he had to step across to the window . . . to seek comfort from the gray sky.

Felice must have been shocked by this image: Franz masturbating as he looked out at the clouds. Next she must have wondered, if he gets an erection thinking about me, why does he keep repeating with such humiliating obstinacy that he will never be able to possess me?

She doesn't quite dare ask him the question. She is unable to speak about sexuality, or to hear it mentioned. Her upbringing, her social class, forbid it. When Franz had spoken, that night at the Brods', about his vacation at Jungborn with the nudists, she had felt gooseflesh: completely naked people, he had said, strolled through the trees, stretched, ran, scratched themselves, stroked their naked bodies. The picture still made her sick, even these many months later. Franz, to his eternal credit, made a point of saying that he always wore his bathing suit.

In the next weeks, the more Franz castigates himself, the more Felice refuses to understand what he is talking about. He begs her: "Don't shut your eyes, don't give in to illusions, I will never change. My need to keep up an uninterrupted exchange of letters with you comes not from love but from my unhappy disposition."

She swears that if she continues to write him, it is not—as he thinks—out of pity. She is bound to him.

Tired of wrangling, they pass on to other subjects. The talk is of the incidents of daily life, of friends, books, the weather. Felice has promised to take swimming lessons, Franz is unhappy that she is making no progress. He asks her: "Are you learning with the help of a pole or do they have you on an apparatus?"

He describes his new neighbor to her, a Czech who writes erotic novels, a splendid and enviable man with a natty little French goatee, a slouch hat straight from Montmartre, and a cape draped over his arm. On another day, he mentions that he broke his fine shaving mirror. It made him shake with annoyance.

Felice has toothaches, Franz is worried. On the day of the extraction, he is anxious and cannot sleep. One's head spins.

The Triumph of Time and Disillusion[5]

T ruly, everything is as it was. Please don't worry un-
necessarily," Felice writes, exasperated by Franz's
insistence. "Everything is as it was" has a wonderful
ring to it, but Franz is convinced of the contrary, even
when Felice manages to shake his firmest convictions. He
has tried to push her away in the hopes of sparing her
greater suffering. He has failed. He is thoroughly relieved—
he would have been destroyed if she had expelled him
("expelled" is the term he uses), and he is distraught that

---

5 Title of an oratorio by Handel.

she has not done so. He struggles with his anxiety attacks and his fits of despair. He could have built the pyramids, he jokes, with the effort it takes him "to cling to life and reason."

To settle his nerves, he decides to take a practical course in gardening. Manual labor calms him, as he knows. A year or two earlier, he had tried his hand at carpentry. The experiment had been a success. He liked everything about the work, from the smell of the wood chips to the rasp of the saw. The workshop had been flooded with light, the craftsmen calm, sturdy people, intent on their tasks, taciturn but good company. Only the press of other obligations had made Franz give it up.

At the end of the workday he goes for the first time to Nusle, a lively suburb of Prague. He discovers, on stepping off the tram, a neighborhood of modest houses surrounded by open and unfenced vegetable gardens. There is a great deal going on around him. Children are playing in the streets, fighting over American swings, young girls are singing next to a merry-go-round, somewhere a brass band is playing, workingmen on their way home talk in clusters and drink beer, while others hoe their garden plots.

The vegetable gardener is waiting for him in front of his land at the appointed place. He hands Franz a spade and shows him how to use it, to spread his legs slightly and bend his knees, lean forward from the waist, keep the neck relaxed.

"Use the spade as a lever, uproot the whole thing."

The man looks at his pupil's white, slender hands and thinks that he's an idle fellow, unlikely to stay the course.

"Small motions, slower, you don't want to hurt your back. Drive the spade with your foot."

Franz is wearing only a shirt and trousers. It is cold, and a fine April rain falls intermittently. He continues assailing and moving the heavy soil all the same. Soon he is sweating and developing blisters on his hands, but he feels a happy fatigue. "This dull, honest, useful, silent, solitary, healthy, strenuous work," he writes Felice that evening, "is not without significance to someone who has led a desk-and-sofa life, allowing himself continually to be assailed and deeply moved." On subsequent days the crunching sound of the earth stays in his ears.

His body becomes heavier, straighter, his sense of his own dignity is reinforced. "I feel," he writes to Max, "like a Fury that has been tamed."

He breathes more easily because Felice has not replaced him. He was so frightened! On a business trip to Frankfurt, she attended a trade exhibition where she came in contact with a great many people and answered none of his letters. Franz imagined that she had met a vigorous, well-dressed, healthy, and amusing young man who took his place. He went through the hell of being abandoned. He panicked, ran to his good friend Max: "Please write to Felice, I absolutely must know."

The fear of losing her was strangling him. The next day he received a few words from her. Life returned.

"Love me a little, Felice. Do you feel how much I love you? Do you feel it?" he writes, forgetting the thousand warnings he has given her.

Subsequently, he asks for, he insists on, a second meeting in Berlin at Whitsun, in mid-May.

"I must, must, see you, Felice."

He agrees to everything. Meet her parents? At home? Attend the reception they are giving for the engagement of her brother, Ferry? Good idea. Everything seems like a good idea.

He is already concerned about the clothes he will wear on his visit: a black suit? He would feel more comfortable in his normal summer suit.

"Should I bring flowers for your mother? And what kind of flowers?"

A stream of questions. He returns to the subject so often after Felice no longer wants to discuss it, directs her so insistently to think more deeply about it, that Felice starts writing less often. In her short, laconic letters, he sees only the words "in haste" and "again in haste."

"My eyes hurt at the very sight of these words."

"You're the one hurting me, I am sad and tired," she answers.

Sad and tired. How could she not be? Franz's indecision, his contradictions, his tyranny, his demands, his complaints have worn her down.

By introducing him to her family, the young woman is leading him toward marriage, and he knows it. For the moment, he is preoccupied with one thing only: Felice has not thought enough, or perhaps not thought at all, about the confession he sent her. Her quick dismissal of it obsesses him, casts a pall on their future.

What does he expect from her? Either she must drive him from her life or else accept the prospect of marriage without coitus, free him from an obligation he feels unable to meet. He even suggests that they not live in the same city. Discussing this with her is the real reason for the second meeting.

He arrives in Berlin early on the morning of Sunday, May 11, 1913. He will leave again on Monday, May 12, in the evening. It is Whitsun, the weather mild and spring-like. He arrives at the home of Carl and Anna Bauer in the middle of the afternoon. His knees wobbling, he walks across their drawing room toward Felice. A shudder of aversion runs through him. He sees gold gleaming in his beloved's mouth as she opens it to greet him: "this gleaming gold, a truly hellish luster for this inappropriate spot, and that grayish yellow porcelain" horrify him. He lowers his eyes, wants only to escape. At that precise moment, he feels with certainty through his whole body that no, he will never be able to possess this young woman.

There are many people in the drawing room. Franz is in such a state of confusion that he is persuaded the people around him are giants, shaking their heads in resignation at his own small size. Felice, in high spirits, flits from person to person. The moment she stands next to Franz, her liveliness fades, her gaze wanders, she endures his silence or the stupid things he has to say. She finds that he looks unwell.

"You seem exhausted," she says.

He doesn't hear her. The suspicious glances that Frau Bauer casts at him frighten him particularly. Dressed all in black, sad, watchful, stiff, a stranger among her own family and friends, Frau Bauer looks disapprovingly, almost contemptuously, at the strange specimen her daughter has brought home. A man who seems ill at times, at others absent, dumb mostly.

Then all at once, before the copious buffet laid out in the dining room, before the astonished guests, Franz stops being tongue-tied. In an excited voice, he tells the gathering about his vegetarianism. He pointedly helps himself to just a few vegetables, drinks only water. Only Erna, Felice's sister, shows any sympathy. The others turn their backs on him.

Noticing the vacuum he has created around himself, Franz senses disaster. He has not managed to steal even a quick kiss from Felice, and she has hardly given him the chance. When, haggard and crestfallen, Franz decides to leave the reception, Felice accompanies him as far as the hall. Franz grabs her hand, pulls off her glove, and kisses her bare palm. He thinks he sees an angry frown on the young woman's face. He flees, his head reels, something in his breast is breaking.

The next morning, they meet alone in the street for a few minutes. Felice, distracted and in a bad mood, has no idea where she stands. Her parents, her brother, her close relatives, her friends were all eager to meet this young man "of the two hundred letters" who was dying of love. What they saw was a ghost. They barely hide their disappointment. Standing stiffly on the sidewalk, her face a mask, her eyes avoiding his, Felice is clearly bored. Franz, at a loss, can't find the words he came to say.

"I cannot live without her. Nor can I live with her." This thought runs through his head as he throws his clothes into his bag. He is back in his room at the Hotel Askanischer Hof, preparing to return to Prague. He cannot possess this woman, but he wishes that he were entirely within her, or she within him. The separation into two people is unbearable.

Once more at home, he writes her the next morning and almost every day thereafter (May 12, 13, 16, 18, 23, 24, 25, 27, and 28). He also writes her almost every day in June (June 1, 2, 6, 7, 10, 13, 15, 16, 17, 19, 20, 22, 23, 26, 27, 28, and 29). In July he writes her another sixteen letters. All of them urge her to reflect on the situation more, to be franker, more mature. He mentions glancingly, in the last line at the bottom of a page, a detail of negligible importance: "I am correcting the page proofs for the first chapter of my American novel, *The Stoker: A Fragment*, which is about to be published in an inexpensive series, 80 pfennigs."

"But," he adds, "the moment I talk about anything other than you, I feel lost."

Not only has Felice made no comment to him about his texts, she has not even mentioned the articles in the German press praising his writings. He is forced to ask her to obtain them for him in the hopes that she will read the reviews and think more highly of his talents as a writer.

She is clearly tired of hearing about his terrible confession, and appears not to believe a word he says, to the point of completely ignoring his finely wrought and stubbornly presented arguments. Is she no longer reading his letters?

On June 16 there is an arresting new development. After laying out interminable arguments, he asks her for the first time, "Do you wish to be my wife? Do you?"

These two question marks seem to leave him stunned. He is unable to write another word that day, the next, or the day after. Apparently destroyed by the proposal, it is only on the fourth day following that he is able to resume his question to the woman who has been his intended since the moment he first glimpsed her.

He finishes his letter with this strange avowal: "I have to say that I am horribly afraid of our future and of the unhappiness that could result from our life together."

It is clear that he expects his proposal of marriage to draw a refusal. Each of their disastrous meetings in Berlin has persuaded him that Felice is unsure of her feelings toward him. Yet she accepts his proposal. Lower-middle-class girl that she is, she requires that he formally ask her father for her hand, although she is twenty-seven years old. She is absolutely set on observing this convention.

Franz promises several times to write her father but puts off the chore day after day and week after week. He has a more immediate task at hand. Caught short by Felice's acceptance, he starts in on a most unusual trial. Never has a lawyer presenting a brief against himself been more eloquent or offered so many decisive arguments. He must lose this trial on which his future as a writer hangs. His life depends on it.

He starts off pleading his case in a minor key, but the volume increases until it deafens Felice. The young woman has just said, "Yes, I want to be your wife."

He answers, "Then you are prepared in spite of everything to take up this cross, Felice? Attempt the impossible?"

"Yes, you will make a good, kind husband."

"You're wrong, you wouldn't manage to live two days at my side. I am a soft worm crawling on the ground, I am taciturn, unsociable, gloomy, brooding, selfish, and a hypochondriac. Could you bear to lead the life of a monk, as I do? I spend most of my time locked away in my room, or else wandering the streets alone. Could you stand to be completely separated from your parents, your friends, and everyone else, since I cannot conceive of our life together in any other way? I want to spare you unhappiness, Felice. Step out of the accursed circle into which I have forced you, blinded as I was and am by love."

He advances the calamitous fact of his perpetual tiredness. She is strong, does she not recognize that he is in poor health?

"What comes between you and me," he says, "is the doctor. I am frail. Insomnia and constant headaches have robbed me of my strength."

"Don't keep on about it," answers Felice. "Stop tormenting me."

He then writes to her describing what married life will be like: "You won't get much help from me. I leave the office around 3, eat lunch, sleep until 6 or 7, bolt something down, then shut myself in my study. Could you really stand such a husband?"

"Yes."

"Think carefully, Felice, think carefully! You would lose Berlin, the office, the work you enjoy, an existence almost free of care, life in the bosom of your family. In Prague, a provincial town, you will hear a language you don't speak, you will live in a petit bourgeois household, without any brilliant society, you will have to forgo pretty dresses, travel third class, sit in poor seats at the theater."

He warns her of another danger: since the only good in him is literature, he will spend their free time, their nights, and their vacations at his writing, leaving her to be alone.

"I know your inclination for writing."

"My inclination?" (He chokes with indignation.) "My inclination? I hate everything that is not literature! If I had to stop writing, I would stop living."

Tired of the abuse, Felice interrupts this useless and exhausting correspondence. They have agreed on nothing when, by common consent, they decide to take their vacations separately. She will go north, to the island of Sylt in the Baltic Sea. He will go south, to Italy.

Riva, the Italian Interlude

On September 6, Franz accompanies his director at the Workers' Accident Insurance Institute, Dr. Robert Marschner, to Vienna. Marschner has a very high opinion of his subordinate;[6] and Franz in turn admires him (but then he bows down before everybody!) because the man types so fast and shares his taste for poetry. One day, while callers waited in the hallway for their

---

6 Several texts written by Kafka on insurance coverage in the building industry and accident prevention in the workplace have survived.

appointments, Franz and Robert read poems aloud behind the closed door of the office.

Spending a week together, they visited the International Congress for First Aid and Accident Prevention. Also taking place on September 6 was the Eleventh Zionist Congress, attended by the daughter of Theodor Herzl. Franz sat in on a few sessions out of curiosity. He left them disappointed, having heard only the usual shrill arguments. To Max, a militant Zionist, he sends a dispiriting account.

On September 14 he leaves Vienna, a city he dislikes. "It is a vast, moribund village," he writes, "where the gay become morose and the morose even moroser."

Finally on vacation, he spends a night alone in Trieste and proceeds to Venice by boat. Crossing in a gale, he is seasick, and it is raining hard when he lands in the City of the Doges. Wet through and through, he runs from church to church, barely able to see the facades of the palaces, hidden as they are behind sheets of gray water. He spends two melancholy days there. In Verona it is even worse. He is surrounded by entwined couples. "The idea of a honeymoon," he writes to Max Brod, "fills me with horror. Couples are an odious sight to me. If I want to make myself sick, I have only to imagine myself with a woman, my arm around her waist."

He seeks refuge in a cinematograph theater, perhaps the Pathé di San Sebastiano, and the film that he sees (he doesn't give its title) brings tears to his eyes.

From this city of lovers, he sends a few lines that he thinks might be the last: "What are we to do, Felice? We must part ways."

Now to the interlude.

An Italian interlude on the magical shores of Lake Garda at Riva. It is a warm, luminous autumn, the water and the parks are soft in color, lightly veiled in mist. Franz has taken up residence at a sanatorium that offers hydrotherapy treatments under Dr. von Hartungen. Along the lakeshore are deck chairs, where guests spend endless hours in the sun. Franz goes for a long swim every day, often to one of the nearby islands.

Meals are taken communally around a large table. Forced to make conversation with his neighbor, a retired general who peppers him with questions, Franz's feelings of emptiness and grief grow more acute.

At the start of the second week, a young girl, her auburn hair tied back in a red ribbon, takes a seat beside him at lunch. She wears a garnet-colored velvet dress, set off by a white lace collar, and has the fragility, the troubling innocence, of a child. When Franz, suddenly voluble, asks her questions, her round cheeks and neck turn red. He is fascinated by the perfection and whiteness of her teeth, the softness of her skin, he longs to untie the ribbon and touch the hair that falls to her shoulders.

She is a foreigner, Swiss-born, living in Genoa. Very thin and graceful, immature, Gerti Wasner is so lovely, her every feature so delicate: her wrists, her ankles, the oval of her face, the shadow of her long eyelashes. She is so unlike sturdy, homely Felice, so young, so divinely young, that Franz never leaves her side. They row together on the lake, Franz at the oars. He is dazzled by Gerti, her deep voice, green eyes, perpetually bright gaze. They walk along the shore. At naptime they lower themselves into adjoining deck chairs. He tells her about Felice and their breakup, about his humdrum existence in Prague. One day he reads to her. He knows by experience how susceptible young women are to his voice, to the eyes he raises to check that they are falling into his net, and remaining prisoners there. He has chosen to read *The Queen of Spades* to her.

"Who is this Alexander Sergeyevich Pushkin?" the girl asks when he closes the book.

She knows nothing about the writer and wants to learn everything. Franz also likes to know every aspect of the lives of famous men. He tells Gerti about the poet's origins, about Gannibal, his Ethiopian great-grandfather, a black man in white Russia who was also Tsar Peter's godson.

He recites some of his favorite lines from Pushkin's poetry, from *The Stone Guest*, from "The Bronze Horseman." There are so many, and each is in a different style. He describes Pushkin's brilliant life, his literary triumphs, his political exiles, and his death, that tragic duel.

"Why? With whom?"

"Pushkin had an exceedingly beautiful wife, Natalya Goncharova. A splendid name, don't you agree?"

He repeats it, savoring each syllable.

"D'Anthès, a French aristocrat, made love to her too openly, and Pushkin's jealous heart took exception to it. There was a duel. D'Anthès pierced his lung. He lay for forty-six hours on his deathbed while the people of Saint Petersburg prayed for him under his window. He died in horrible agony, his last words being: 'My life is over. It hurts to breathe.' He was thirty-eight years old."

Gerti is moved. So is Franz. Young girls have always had a strange power over him. They affect him because it is their fate to become women and lose their beauty, their innocent grace. He cannot help admiring a young girl who deserves it and loving her until his admiration runs out.

He wants to know everything about Gerti: about her, her family, Switzerland, Genoa. He is attentive to her slightest wishes, and so thoughtful that the young girl discovers and explores the limits of her power. They revel in the desire that each provokes in the other.

Since meeting her, Franz is no longer the same man. He jokes, invents stories, does imitations of the other guests, mimics the quavering voice of the retired general. Gerti laughs, her head tipped back. For the first time, he writes, he understands a Christian girl and lives almost entirely within the sphere of her influence.

The sphere of her influence? Is he referring to the games Gerti suggests, in which he good-naturedly takes part, however childish they might seem? At night, when each has retired, Gerti, who lives in the room above Franz, lets down a long ribbon, which Franz grasps. They both lean far out of their windows to catch a glimpse of each other. Some nights, Franz knocks on the ceiling and waits for Gerti's answering knock. Lying motionless on his bed, his ears cocked, he hears her walk overhead, hum, cough. He follows her every movement until she falls asleep.

They have only ten days. Then they will go their separate ways, and it will all be over. A love without future, without anxiety, without physical embrace, a chaste love, with glances that penetrate and make them almost tremble. Franz has known a similar enchantment only once before, one long-ago summer: her name was Selma, she was fifteen, he seventeen.

Gerti knows that Franz is a writer. One day he asks if she likes fairy tales, he would like to write some for her. He doesn't tell her that at that moment he is imagining her sitting in the dining room, hiding his tales in her lap under the table. He sees her reading between courses and blushing horribly. Horribly? Why? Is he thinking of ribald tales?

Gerti refuses his offer outright. She makes him promise three things: "We will never see each other again. We will never write each other, not even a single line. And you will neither write nor say anything about me."

Franz kept his word. He always refused to answer any of Max's questions about her. In his *Diaries*, he wrote only the girl's initials, GW (from which her identity was only discovered decades later).

The little that we know of this brief encounter comes from his *Diaries*, where the events of these two weeks take up barely ten lines, and from the letter he writes to Felice three months later, on December 29, when he confesses to his fiancée, with his usual abrupt frankness, that he fell in love with a young Swiss woman, almost a child, eighteen years old, that he was very attached to her, but that they had not been right for each other. On the day of his departure, he says, the young woman almost burst into tears, and he was just as bad.

Yet this episode convinced him that deep inside, what he truly aspired to was . . . to marry Felice.

He carried away from his stay in Riva one regret. The ribbon games that he played with Gerti prevented him from taking his pleasure with the young Russian woman in the room directly across the hall from his. Each of her smiles, each of her innuendos, had been an invitation.

Franz leaves Riva a little surer of himself. His hair is starting to turn gray, his eyes are gentler.

Grete Bloch, or the First Trio

Felice is the one who, after two months, decides to break the silence, a silence that is starting to feel like a final separation. In her letter dated October 23, 1913, she informs Franz that a friend of hers is coming to Prague, a young woman, whom she has charged with effecting their reconciliation. Furthermore, she asks Franz to come to Berlin in the days after the meeting.

Franz has received three letters from Felice's unknown friend, three letters that he has left unanswered. How could Felice ever imagine that an emissary coming out of the blue, totally ignorant of their complicated history, could magically sort out their differences? How could she ever have hoped such a thing?

The idea of explaining himself to this unknown lady, who was most likely of a certain age, tall, strong, and maternal, does not appeal to him.

Even as he tells himself he won't go, a temptation arises: to introduce a new element or character, however secondary, into a plot that has stalled, and onto a stage that is emptying. He wants to break the monotony of the passing days. His life was starting to feel like one of those schoolboy punishments where you are made to write the same absurd sentence a hundred times.

Who is this woman friend that Felice is sending me, though she has never spoken of her before? After a few days of hesitation, he answers Fräulein Grete Bloch: "Certainly I shall come to your hotel, please name a convenient time."

And to Felice: "Since you have requested it, I shall arrive in Berlin on Saturday, November 8, and leave the next day between 4 and 5 o'clock."

A useless trip, he knows, another trip that will bring no added light, no final resolution to their conflict. In the meantime, typically enough, he starts to ask himself questions: How did Grete Bloch get drawn into this mission? What does she expect from it? Where does she live? In what quarter does she stretch her limbs before going to sleep? Could I ever do what she is doing? What would I feel? What will happen to her when she gets older? These thoughts agitate him, and he gets a stomachache.

He meets Fräulein Grete Bloch on November 1, 1913, in the lobby of her hotel, The Black Horse. He doesn't like the look of her and is suspicious from the outset. She is wearing a showy fur stole that doesn't suit her. Franz has a fierce aversion to fur, this one especially, with its long guard hairs and silk lining.

But Fräulein Grete Bloch is not a matron. She is a frail young woman, somewhat unusual looking, much younger than Felice. Twenty years old? Thin lips, an intelligent face. She looks up at him with melancholy eyes, is deferential toward him, which he responds to.

When she urges him to make the trip to Berlin, which she describes as absolutely essential, he objects: "Both my trips there have been a disaster. After each of our meetings, Felice has felt more hesitant than ever."

Fräulein Grete Bloch smiles. "Perhaps, Dr. Kafka, you should write to her less and visit her more?"

As they part, he eagerly agrees to the meeting she proposes for the following day. He adds, "Fräulein, may I write you in Vienna? Your mission is not over."

Immediately on his return from Berlin on November 10, 1913, Franz sends the young woman a letter. He is writing her, he mentions straight off, even before writing to Felice. This declaration is so flattering that Felice's friend perhaps slides unawares down the slope of ambiguity. He tells her in abundant detail about his recent encounter with Felice. He writes Fräulein Bloch again the next day and on the following days without giving her time to answer. It is true that Felice is at the heart of these first letters: he hopes to learn from Grete what his fiancée's secret intentions are, as well as what lies behind her hesitations and her silence.

Since his visit to Berlin, Franz has received nothing further from Felice. His letters and telegrams remain unanswered. On the telephone, she promises to write him that same day, but nothing comes of it. Franz asks his mother to send her a note. Still nothing. He then asks his friend, Dr. Ernst Weiss, who lives in Berlin, to visit Felice at her office and prod her out of her silence. Franz receives a five-word letter: "I will write you soon." He sends her four telegrams, gets four categorical promises in return, including this one: "My letter has been mailed." Nothing comes. "It's inhuman," he tells her. He sends her three more letters, receives none in return. He then questions Grete: "Do you know anything, and would you be willing to tell me?"

He is thoroughly confused, all the more so because he and his parents are moving. They are relocating to the Oppelt house. Everything is topsy-turvy. He sleeps miserably and works too hard. At half past midnight on a freezing night, his feet bundled in a blanket, he writes once more to Felice, imploring her: "Say 'yes' or 'no,' it will cost you no effort. Don't call me 'dear' if you don't love me, don't send me affectionate regards if that's not what they are. Just a short letter. This is not too much to ask. Even if you should leave me no hope, I will continue to wait for you. By asking you to write, I am causing you much suffering, but not nearly as much as your silence causes me. Do you not think that I am worth at least a word?"

Felice's silence makes him turn his attention toward Grete. It is to her that he now sends his thoughts, to her that he poses innumerable questions. It is also to his "Dear Fräulein Grete" that he offers reams of advice. About her health regimen: perform exercise regularly, learn to swim, sleep with the window open, stop taking valerian, eat at vegetarian restaurants (there are some excellent ones near you), chew each bite of food for five minutes before swallowing. About her work. And about Vienna: leave that city as soon as possible, return to Berlin. He waits for her answers with almost the same fever he feels when

Felice's letters arrive late. He asks Grete to come to Berlin when he is there, offers to meet her at some halfway point, so great is his desire to see her.

He advances further into ambiguous territory. When he learns that Grete was born on March 21, he calls her "Child of Spring." He asks her for several photographs of herself and her friends.

During the year 1914, he writes Felice about twenty letters, whereas he writes more than seventy to Grete. He feels strongly drawn to her and, honest with himself, he does not deny the fact. This epistolary relationship, this new intrigue, gives him stability and security.

But while he is playing havoc with Grete's heart, he is clinging to Felice. The more she hesitates and the more she holds him at arm's length, the more he pressures her to decide. He says, "I can't live without you, you just as you are."

During the night of Friday, February 27, 1914, he abruptly decides to make a surprise visit to Felice in Berlin. On Saturday morning, he steps off the train and heads for Felice's office, where he has never been. He waits at the switchboard while a secretary goes to tell Felice of his arrival. He is happy to be there. Felice arrives, quite surprised by this unexpected visit, but greets him in a friendly way. They stand and talk for a few moments, then Felice returns to her office, where a number of people are waiting to see her. The two meet at noon at a pastry shop and spend an hour together. He accompanies her back to the office, because he is keen to see the room where she works. Late in the afternoon, they meet again and stroll together for two hours. Felice is busy that night. There is a ball she must attend for her work.

"Don't go, let's spend the evening together. We still have so many knots to untangle."

"I can't turn down the invitation at the last moment. That's impossible. Let's see each other tomorrow, I'm free all morning."

On Sunday they stroll arm in arm through the Tiergarten like the happiest of engaged couples, then stop for refreshments in a cafe where they run into Dr. Weiss. Felice frowns at the sight of him. She has tried to convince Franz more than once that Ernst Weiss is hateful, and Ernst Weiss has tried more than once to convince Franz that Felice is hateful.

As she takes her leave, Felice solemnly promises Franz that she will accompany him to the station at the end of the afternoon.

On the platform he cranes his neck to catch a glimpse of her. The train gets under way. Once more, she has failed to turn up. But she sends a telegram, the excuse is called "Aunt Marta."

Sitting on the wooden seats of a noisy, smelly, poorly heated third-class railway compartment, Franz mulls over every statement Felice made while they strolled in the park. As the train jolts and his head bumps against the frozen windowpane, their dialogue scrolls dizzyingly through his mind.

"I quite like you, Franz, but that's not enough to get married. I don't want to do things by halves."

"But I love you so much that I am ready to marry you even if your feelings toward me are lukewarm. I implore you, Felice, say yes, even if you believe that your feelings for me fall short. My love for you is big enough to make up the difference."

"I have fears about our future together. I worry that I might not be able to put up with your idiosyncrasies, your indecision: what you want now, you no longer want a moment later."

"I am sewn once and for all inside my skin, and nothing can alter my seams."

"With you, it's nothing but surprises and disappointments. I'm afraid that I wouldn't really be able to give up Berlin, my family, the office, buying nice clothes, and going to the theater. I've been thinking about all the arguments you've made repeatedly. You're right, I would have to give up too much. Of the two of us, I would carry the heavier burden."

"What I conclude is that you don't love me at all."

"You're wrong. Look at the locket I wear around my neck. Your picture is with me night and day. I will never marry anyone but you."

"Do you plan to go on writing to me? Or not?"

"You decide. I would be willing to go on writing. But I would also be willing to stop writing you."

"Then it would all be over, and each of us would take back his letters and photographs?"

"No. I would never return your letters or your photographs. I would never throw them away or ask for mine to be returned."

He sees the two of them pacing back and forth along the footpaths of the zoo. He is gesturing and pleading his case, ready to fall at Felice's feet. She appears ready to end the conversation, which she finds annoying.

In front of them, in enormous cages, perched on the branches of a cement tree, monkeys are leaping, chasing each other frenetically. They emit piercing cries, grating one's nerves. He sees the marmosets running in every direction, exhibiting their bright red bottoms and erect members, their long tails swishing through the air.

The lewd behavior of the monkeys, their screams, their mad dashes, their brazen behavior, irritate Felice: "Franz, for the love of God, stop pleading with me. You always want the impossible. Don't attach so much importance to every word."

"You want only to humiliate me!"

"You're the one who is looking for humiliation! The only thing that interests you, as you've said a hundred times, is tormenting others and being tormented! I've had enough of being both your victim and your executioner."

She grows impatient, wants to leave. He restrains her. She responds with a sullen silence, in which hatred and disgust lurk. She looks everywhere but at him, furious.

The film plays over and over in his head, the images become confused, he sees only bright red buttocks. They swirl, fill the whole screen, the cries of the monkeys and of Felice blend together, hammer at his skull, drive him crazy.

Once back in Prague, he makes a decision that helps him ward off the temptation to commit suicide: if he doesn't marry Felice, he will quit his job, leave Prague, move to Berlin, and become a journalist.

In March, Felice appears intent on mending their relationship again.

"Forget the horrid words I said to you in the park, I was overwrought, nervous, and upset about what had happened to my brother Ferry. You know how much I love him, what's happening to him is terrible, I'll tell you when I see you, he had to leave Berlin suddenly. Franz, if you want me, if the love I have for you is enough, I am willing to be your wife. Can you take me as though nothing had happened?"

"Felice, I do take you, with everything that has happened, and I will keep you though I should lose my mind. I love you to the limits of my strength."

They see each other again at Easter for a quiet engagement party. The gathering of the two families occurs in Berlin, at the Bauers' house. Once again, their reunion is short and unhappy. The engaged couple are never alone. Franz doesn't even manage to kiss Felice, who seems not to mind.

She sets the date of their wedding for September.

He is surprised: "Why wait six months? Let's move the wedding forward."

She refuses.

The official announcement of their engagement appears in the daily newspapers in Berlin and Prague. Franz, who composed the announcement, jokes: "Those four lines sound to me like a public announcement, to the effect that, on Whitsunday, F.K. will perform a figure-skating exhibition at the music hall!"

All their subsequent attention is given to organizing the reception, planned for June 1.

On May 6, Felice is in Prague. She visits the latest apartment Franz has found, after combing the city for weeks. She doesn't like it. The couple agree about nothing: neither their choice of furniture nor the life they will lead. Felice insists that Franz eat meat, that he sleep in a room that is adequately heated, that he give more time to the asbestos factory, and that he stop writing at night. The enormous sideboard that she buys frightens Franz. "It is a perfect funeral monument," he says.

His parents are the ones who eventually find him a reasonable apartment and who pay the landlord the first six months' rent.

Will they also lay me in my grave? Franz asks himself.

The closer the date of the official engagement comes, the more he suffers from insomnia, headaches, and nervous attacks.

On May 27, Julie Kafka and her youngest daughter, Ottla, set off for Berlin ahead of the others. Franz and his father are to arrive three days later.

On Whitsun Monday, an elegant reception is held at the Bauers' with a multitude of guests, a sumptuous buffet. But the bride-to-be looks tired, suddenly aged, her skin roughened, blemished. Her teeth, in worse condition than before, are filled with gold. Franz is distracted, agitated, downcast, and slips out onto the balcony to be alone. His face ashen, he feels handcuffed, like a criminal surrounded by policemen. He thinks only of fleeing, somewhere, anywhere, escaping from the trap that he has thrown himself into. He seems not to notice Grete at all or the sad eyes that she lifts toward him.

In the following days, he is incapable of writing to Felice. All his letters are for Grete. He demonstrates to her, in the end convincingly, that he neither wants nor is capable of marrying, that he has no aptitude for marriage, that everything in him revolts against the

proposed union. His letter of July 3 is so clear that Grete
is terrified.

Imagine her feelings, her embarrassment.

What is she to do now that she has heard this terrible,
this magnificent admission? Keep quiet? Warn Felice? Be-
tray her friend? Take her place?

The Trial

On this Sunday, July 12, 1914, it is so fine a day in Berlin that, on stepping off the train, Franz hires a hackney to take him to the Hotel Askanischer Hof, where he is accustomed to staying. Entering the lobby, he is surprised to find Felice. It is the first time that she has come to meet him.

She is not alone.

Her sister Erna, her friend Grete Bloch, and the surgeon Ernst Weiss are grouped around her.

Is it an ambush? he wonders. Grete must have told calumnies about me to Felice, and together they have set a trap for me. He examines them. They look embarrassed and avoid his gaze. Grete nervously mops her neck with a handkerchief. Felice maintains an icy expression. She extends a limp hand to him. Is he no longer allowed to kiss her cheek? Only his friend, Ernst Weiss, seems at ease, as though impatient to operate.

They enter a private conference room and shut the door behind them.

Felice sits across from her fiancé. This long-limbed man, quiet and elegant, irritates her. She runs her fingers through her hair, stifles a yawn, squirms in her chair, and tugs on her skirt, which is pinching her at the waist. She has grown heavier. She reproaches herself for not having followed Dr. Müller's gymnastics regimen for women, which Franz sent her.

She is the first to speak: "It's time to sort things out, Franz. Since May 28, even before our engagement, you have not written me, not a single word. All your letters went to Grete, whose friendship with me you've been trying to wreck. I no longer know where I am in this, or who you are, or who you love, or what game you're playing. Grete and I have decided to ask very specific questions, and to demand very specific answers. Grete, would you go first?"

Unlike Felice, Grete is emotional. Her face is flushed

and she speaks hesitantly, in a choked voice. Her eyes remain glued to the bit of paper in her hand.

"Dr. Kafka, since our meeting in Prague on November 1, you have written me sixty-seven letters. In your most recent letters, you have gone to great lengths to convince me that you cannot possibly marry. Everything in you rebels against such a union. I deeply regret that I insisted on seeing your engagement as a benefit to you both, and deeply regret encouraging you to proceed down that path. In doing so, I assumed an enormous responsibility, which I never should have taken on. And that is why I sent Felice some of your letters. I underlined in red the passages that alarmed me. I couldn't stay silent any longer. I no longer dared look Felice in the eye. My complicity in—"

"Fräulein Bloch," says Ernst Weiss, interrupting, "these letters were addressed to you personally, were they not? Did you ask Dr. Kafka for permission to pass them on to Fräulein Felice Bauer? Did you even warn him that you intended to do it?"

"I warned him. After I sent them."

"You'd known Fräulein Bauer for a long time when she asked you to plead her case?"

"Five months."

"Five months? You live in Vienna and Fräulein Bauer in Berlin, so you can hardly know each other very well.

Yet in spite of that, you agreed to undertake a delicate mission for her?"

Grete makes no answer. Dr. Weiss resumes: "Why did you continue to correspond with Dr. Kafka? You spoke of sixty-seven letters, I believe? And you replied to them? Why did you not end your role as mediator earlier?"

"I didn't, I hoped, Dr. Kafka . . ."

She doesn't complete the sentence. She guiltily remembers sending Dr. Kafka two of Felice's letters to her and trembles at the prospect of exposure. What would her friend do if she found out? It had been easy enough to predict the effect of those two letters on Dr. Kafka. In them, Felice confessed that secretly—but the secret had now been betrayed—she harbored grave doubts about her feelings toward Franz.

Grete says nothing. All eyes turn toward Dr. Kafka. What will he say in response? He mumbles a few barely comprehensible words: "Nothing. True."

Felice upbraids her fiancé: "Oh no, you're not going to sit there and say nothing. That would be too easy!"

She pulls from her purse the incriminating evidence: a wad of letters with passage after passage underlined in red.

"You completely stopped writing me, your fiancée. I became just a pretext for writing to another woman, a woman you seduced shamefully, in every way possible, asking ten thousand questions, about her, her brother, her cat, her mother, her office, her girlfriends, offering ten thousand compliments and pieces of advice. Was it to ask her about me that you wrote in this letter [she reads in a heavily ironic tone]: 'Dear Fräulein Grete, how do you look after your teeth? Do you brush them after each meal?' In this one you call her 'Child of Spring,' you tell her your dreams, you imagine her reclining on a checked bedspread."

She rummages among the papers in front of her. She exclaims, "You were curious about the dress Grete planned to wear at my engagement but showed no interest at all in mine. 'Your dress, dear Fräulein Grete, will be viewed with the most, well, the most affectionate eyes.' You had the nerve to write her that. And this, which is even worse: 'You cannot be fully aware of what you mean to me. I have been actually, visibly languishing for you. Once we are married, you will come and live with us from the very beginning. You shall hold my hand, and I, in order to thank you, must be allowed to hold yours.' And what am I to do while you hold her hand so that you can endure my presence? Am I to watch you lust after another woman? Or am I just to go to the devil?"

How to get out of this room? Franz asks himself, his face ashen. How to get away from this noise, this face distorted by hatred?

He remembers the prostitute he often visits, a big girl in outmoded clothes with fanciful adornments that give her an air of luxury. One night as they were getting dressed, he asked her about her work. He remembers her voice, her Austrian accent. She said that when a client was old, or brutal, or smelly, while he grunted at her ear, his heavy, sweating body glued to hers, she was always able to leave her sagging cot and the man fucking her and the miserable shack where she lived. All she had to do was to imagine a scene, always the same scene, Franz didn't ask what it was, and she would leave her body at its business and sail far away to a place that was always the same, and always magical.

Dissociating oneself. Will I be able to do it too? Did I manage to get away for a few moments from the torrent of reproaches that Felice has been heaping on me? He closes his eyes so as not to see the hellish gleam of gold that glints in her mouth. He hears Felice hammer on but in a muffled voice, as though a heavy curtain had fallen between them: ". . . her photograph, several photographs, not enough for you . . . 'the most charming, the most lovely thing I've ever received! And your portrait, contemplate' . . . from morning to night, and you . . ."

Think about Gerti, he tells himself, about her smile in the canoe. About her ribbons, her childish lips, her long lashes. About our walks.

Words float like clouds, or rather, it is he who floats, far away, out of reach.

". . . You tyrannized me, you tormented me with your doubts, your neurasthenia, you tried to make me adopt your asceticism. And what about your unbelievable behavior before our engagement? How could you let your parents hire a detective to investigate my family's financial situation, their moral standing, and even mine? How can I ever forgive you this despicable lack of trust?"

Her resentment, which has long smoldered, flares out. Speaking energetically, her back straight, she spares her fiancé no details, reminding him of the many daily torments, the tears she has been shedding for months. Before the three dumbstruck judges, she even tosses into the ring the news of her wayward fiancé's transgressions.

He looks at Felice, her dull hair, her stern gaze. What did she say?

"Your affair . . . a child . . . Riva."

"It's time to bring this to a close," says Grete. "You must break off your engagement."

Ernst Weiss, delighted, speaks volubly to this purpose. Erna timidly proposes that a happier outcome might be possible.

Each has spoken. The eyes of the four judges turn toward Dr. Kafka, motionless under the barrage. Around him is a wall of silence. He has folded his arms across his chest. Is he containing the beating of his heart? Petrified, he seems incapable of thinking, looking, speaking, taking part in what is going on around him, which is nothing less than a punishment in the public square.

No one dares break the silence. They are all waiting for him to come back to life.

He rises, and the others follow suit. To everyone's surprise, he walks toward Grete, who has sprung him from his engagement.

"You must hate me," she says.

"You're wrong, and even if the whole world hated you, I would not. You assumed the role of judge, it was horrible for you, for me, for everyone. In reality, I sat in your position, and I sit there permanently. The reproaches that you and Felice heaped on me are ones I have considered a hundred times. But you should not have exhibited my letters. Never would I have exposed yours to others."

"Please give them back. I should get rid of them, I should burn them all."

"No. I am keeping them, but don't worry in the slightest."

He takes his leave of Felice: "You have every right to be angry with me. But why did you subject me to this trial? This public flogging? This humiliation? I felt like a dog!"

That evening, he invites the kind and compassionate Erna to dine with him at the Belvedere, a restaurant along the river.

"I would like to give you some consolation," she says.

"I am not unhappy, or rather, I am unhappy to be as I am, about which I am inconsolable."

"Why did you not defend yourself in front of the others?"

"I had nothing decisive to say."

He hums a tune from *Carmen*, "a closed mouth, no fly can enter."

"And it's possible," he continues, "that if I had had anything decisive to say, I'd have kept my silence. As an act of defiance."

"Why?"

"All was lost. I could see Felice's unhappiness. She isn't to blame. For two years, she has suffered on my account as no criminal should ever have to suffer. She couldn't understand that for me, the only escape from hell is through literature. But let's leave all that."

He orders wine and, for himself, a slice of roast beef, thick and cooked rare. Erna voices her surprise: "I thought you were a vegetarian. Felice has so often complained of it!"

"She insisted that I eat meat. Despite all the pressure that she brought to bear, I never did give in. I've always made a point of evading power, all forms of power. At my parents' table, I don't eat as they do, I eat in rebellion against them! And yet tonight, with you, I am becoming a carnivore again. And I am drinking wine. Strange as it seems, setbacks actually make me stronger."

"What did you do this afternoon, after . . . ?"

"After the trial at the hotel? I went to the Stralauer Ufer swimming pool. I saw men there with powerful bodies, running madly. I swam for a long time. I lay on the deck in the sun and felt the ebb and flow of tiredness in my joints."

Touched, Erna smiles. "Are you leaving tomorrow night?"

"Yes. Would you like me to pass through Berlin again on my way back from Lübeck? I'd so like to see you again! We could go to Potsdam together. In the meantime, would you give me permission to write you?"

The next morning he sends a letter of farewell by messenger to Carl and Anna Bauer, Felice's parents. That evening, Erna accompanies Franz to the train station. With a troubling expression, she offers him her hand, says she believes in him and still has confidence in him. He is gladdened by her words.

"I'll write you from Lübeck," he promises.

He would wait two weeks before making a brief, elliptical allusion in his *Diaries* to what he always referred to afterward as the "Askanischer Hof Trial."

Two weeks during which he would ruminate the humiliation he suffered on that day. It was as if the shame of it would outlive him.

Humiliation. The theme of the novel that he starts to write.

That Night, or the Marienbad Enigma

He spends two weeks on the beach in Marielyst, Denmark, barefoot, in the company of Ernst Weiss and his mistress Rahel Sansara, after meeting the couple by chance in Lübeck. The bickering of the two lovers sometimes annoys him. The hotel is only adequate. Meals don't extend to fruits or vegetables, so he eats only meat, it's horrible, he feels sick. But the beach is almost deserted, the days are sun-filled, the three of them go swimming every day.

There is a photograph of Franz sitting cross-legged on the sand. Next to the bearlike Ernst Weiss, he appears an adolescent—sullen, distracted, aimless. From morning to night he mulls over the reproaches flung at him by Felice. The humiliation she inflicted on him in public still burns, as though he had rolled in nettles. He is at times relieved to have escaped marriage, at times dispirited at having lost his fiancée. He feels as hollow, he says, as a seashell about to be crushed under his big toe.

On his return trip he stops in Berlin. According to plan, he sees Erna, who proves as amiable as ever.[7] They visit Sanssouci Palace in Potsdam, linger in Voltaire's bedroom, and generally get along so well that they decide to travel together at Christmas.

On Sunday, July 26, 1914, Franz arrives back in Prague, where the mobilization of the military is under way. Disappointed at being turned down for military service—a stint in the army would have freed him from the office, from Prague, from his listlessness—Franz pays little attention to the declarations of war, the troop movements, and the mad bloodthirst intensifying in Europe, as the floodgates of evil prepare to open.

On August 2, learning of Austria's entry into the war, he spends the afternoon at the swimming pool.

---

7 None of Kafka's letters to Erna has survived.

He looks on disparagingly at military parades, "among the most repulsive accompaniments to the hostilities." A cold, often cynical observer, he lambasts "the stupidity of the soldiers, the criminal blindness of the crowd."

His brother-in-law, by contrast, is called up to serve his country. Franz's sister Elli decides to move back in with her parents, along with her two children, Felix and Gerti. Franz turns over his room in his parents' house to his sister and moves into her old apartment.

For the first time in his life, he has a place to himself, a quiet three-bedroom. His routine is as inflexible as ever: at the office until 2:30 p.m., lunch at his parents' house, then home to read the newspaper and the day's mail, followed by a long siesta until 9:00 p.m. He then walks to his parents' for a family dinner and at 10 p.m. rides the tram home. Chained to his desk, he then works on his new novel until he drops from exhaustion. He glimpses Max for a few minutes on his way home from work but no one else. His novel progresses so well that he asks for a week's vacation in October, followed by a second week. He works until five in the morning, sometimes even until 7:30. It is his way of fighting. Absorbed in the pleasure of writing, he is metamorphosed. In the afternoon he indulges in long solitary walks along the paths of Chotek

Park, the most lovely spot in Prague, with its birds, its palace and arcades, its old trees that cling to their last year's leaves, its half-light. He wolfs down a story by Strindberg, *Entzweit*, a gem.[8]

Before long, he is reading Max the first chapter of *The Trial*, and he sends an inventory of the texts he has been working on: "Memories of the Kalda Railway," "The Village Schoolmaster," "The Substitute." "Here I am," he says, "with five or six stories lined up before me like horses in front of a circus ringmaster." He finishes only "In the Penal Colony" and the last chapter of *Amerika*: "The Oklahoma Theater."

No news of Felice since the "Askanischer Hof Trial." He doesn't seek her out. In late October, he receives a letter from her, another letter of regret: regret at having been hostile, nervous, and at the end of her strength.

"Can you explain to me," she writes, "what your position was? What it is today?"

---

8 The Strindberg work published in 1909 in Munich as *Entzweit* is a no-vella known in English as "The Doctor's Second Story," from the Swedish author's collection *Fair Haven and Foul Strand*.

The balance of power has shifted. Now, it is Felice who is begging Franz to write.

He spends several evenings answering her. Reading the many pages he produced, one senses a change, hears a certain weariness, as though Franz were a teacher patiently addressing a student whom a fly has distracted.

"For me, nothing has changed in the last three months, absolutely nothing, either for good or ill, you are still the greatest friend to my work and its greatest enemy."

He explains that there are two beings at war within him: one is more or less congruent with the man that Felice would like to marry, and this man loves her beyond all measure; the other fights against her tooth and nail because of the hatred and fear she feels toward his work and his way of life. And nothing about either one of these men can be changed without destroying both.

He adds: "If I said nothing at the Askanischer Hof, it's because I couldn't shake from my mind your aversion to the way I organize my life."

And he has a duty to protect his work, which alone gives him the moral right to live.

"Our letters never benefited us much," he writes. "Even the most beautiful contained a hidden worm; I'll write you infrequently, we must not start torturing each other again."

Fewer than thirty letters and postcards are exchanged in 1915. But there is again talk of a meeting, again talk of getting married. On January 23 and 24, they rendezvous at a halfway point, in Bodenbach. Felice had gone to the trouble of getting herself a passport. She was forced to make a long detour and spend a sleepless night on the train.

Now they are face to face. She wears a jacket that he finds very handsome. Each of them notices that the other has not changed. In the hours they spend together, they pick up their discussion where they left off before the breakup. Neither will budge. Felice still insists on a comfortable apartment, one to which she can bring her personal taste (he trembles at the idea), ample meals (it could be worse), with bedtime at 11:00 p.m. (out of the question) and a heated bedroom (he is already suffocating). To demonstrate that reason is on her side, she adjusts Franz's watch to the correct time: "Setting a watch an hour and a half ahead makes no sense," she says. "It's absurd."

She asks him not a single question about his work. Nothing. Not a word. And he relents not a bit in his demands. All day they talk at cross-purposes. That night, each retires to bed alone. They occupy adjoining rooms, with a key on either side of the door. At a moment when Franz is experiencing nothing but boredom and emptiness, Felice cries out: "How happy we are together here!"

Not knowing what to do to occupy the hours they must still spend together, Franz reads her the first chapters of *The Trial*. She listens and says nothing, lying on the sofa with her eyes closed. She asks him blandly if she can take the manuscript home to transcribe. She had hoped for something more than this endless reading aloud.

They part.

We have not spent one good moment together, not one minute of total freedom, he tells himself on the train that carries him home. Each of them loves the other just as he or she is, but neither believes, given the other's nature, that they could ever live together.

On May 24, four months later, there is a second meeting in Bohemian Switzerland. It is Whitsuntide, Felice arrives in the company of Grete Bloch (is this not odd?) and her sister Erna, who has recently married. Franz (wanting to leave a record?) sends Ottla a postcard with his signature and those of the three women accompanying him.

The following month, in June, they meet again, this time—at Franz's behest—alone. Little has survived of these two days in Carlsbad: Felice sings several songs for Franz, her voice remarkably true. He in turn hums "À Batignolles," his favorite French song. Once more, Paris casts its spell on him.

In 1916 the rhythm of their correspondence picks up. He writes to Felice several times a week, almost always on a postcard. Letters, which have to be censored by the military authorities, would take weeks to arrive. With the war on, Franz has hardly a moment to himself. "Even more responsibilities, more worries, more insomnia, more headaches (brief dagger thrusts above and to the right of my eye)," that is the tenor of his life now. The management of the wretched asbestos factory has fallen to his lot, as the brother-in-law who ran it has been drafted. At the office, for lack of personnel, his hours have increased. He now works eight hours a day. And to crown it all, his father makes him help out in the store, since most of the employees are at the front. He works hard from morning till night. He no longer has a second to himself, or the strength to write. He is desperate, a rat in a cage.

In April, tired of reading letters that don't lead to anything, Felice asks to see him. Cautious, Franz warns, "Think back to our earlier meetings, and you'll stop wanting another."

He announces his intention of spending the summer vacation in Marienbad, an incredibly beautiful place with large and handsome forests on all sides. He often goes there for business, only last month he was there again. Felice proposes it as a meeting place.

"I am in extraordinary agreement," he answers.

On the evening of July 1, he has the great pleasure of closing his files, dictating a few final memoranda, saying good-bye to one and all, and leaving his office in impeccable good order.

In Marienbad, Felice is waiting for him at the station. His room at the Hotel Neptun, though, is hideous and looks onto a courtyard. Things are starting off badly. The first night is one of distress. The next day, both are determined to make their stay a success, and they move into a palace, the Hotel Schloss Balmoral. There, Franz is given a large and lovely room. But their quarrels ruin everything. To escape the cul-de-sac they are in, they walk a great deal, at times under the pouring rain, at times under clearing skies. He amuses himself by reading the Bible.

He tries to restrict his conversations with Felice to one subject that excites him beyond measure: the Jewish People's Home in Berlin, founded in May by Siegfried Lehmann, Max Brod, and Martin Buber. He urges Felice so insistently to become a teacher there that she agrees to consider the possibility. Franz is elated and immediately asks Max to send her a prospectus. The organization is designed to promote greater contact between Eastern and Western Jews, and to provide an education to the orphaned children pouring into Berlin from Russia and Poland.

Franz encourages Felice: "There is more honey to be drawn from this work than from all the flowers in the forests of Marienbad."

On July 8, they go to Tepl, where Franz has a lawsuit to settle for work. Their relations continue to be abysmal. From the little town, where they spend only a few hours, Franz finds the time to scribble a line or two to Max: "What a creature I am! What a creature I am! I torture her—and torture myself—to death!"

On July 9, nothing has changed, the clouds have not parted—how could they? And yet, after a series of horrible days and worse nights, a miracle occurs. They live airy days together such as Franz had never thought to see again.

They get along so well, they feel so strong in their love, that on July 10 Franz writes—it must be at Felice's request—to Frau Bauer. Once again he has the right to call her "Dear Mother." He announces the "assurance for the future" of his relationship with Felice.

On July 12, he sends a message to Ottla that things are going much better between him and Felice.

The next day, they go to Franzensbad, a spa near Marienbad where Julie Kafka is taking the waters with her daughter, Valli.

"We will get married as soon as the war ends and we will live in a suburb of Berlin," he announces. The interview with his mother, at which Felice is also present, proceeds so perfectly smoothly . . . that it terrifies him.

What has happened? The several-page letter that he sends Max (his confidant) on July 12 gives some insight. His fear of seeing Felice in her full "reality" (should we read "nudity"?) has evaporated. He has realized that he didn't know her at all, that she was reaching out to him. He has accepted her help. He has entered into a relationship with his fiancée such as he has never known before. Once in her intimacy, he saw the confident gaze of a woman.

"How beautiful the softened glow of her eyes, this blossoming from the well of womanhood. I have no right to resist it. For the first time I believe in the possibility of married life," he writes.

Such reserve in telling his story! Such difficulty in saying that the locks had popped! They made love.

For the first time? We don't know. What is certain is that Felice gave him confidence that night. He overcame his fear of the "long, narrow, terrible slit." He discovered, he would say, the beauty of the slim, noble body of his fiancée. And the same pleasures seem to have been renewed on the following nights. Five days of happiness.

Felice returns to Berlin on July 14. He remains in Marienbad alone until July 24. Though he complains of violent headaches, he is calmer, more relaxed, more sensual, quicker, more decisive. He advises his uncle to spend his vacation in Marienbad, a place as peaceful as the Garden after the expulsion of man. He sends him, along with a guidebook to the city, a list of good things and good places: "Take breakfast at the Dianahof (sweetened milk, eggs, honey, butter), grab a bite at the Maxtal (curdled milk), lunch briefly at the Neptun, eat fruits at the greengrocer's, take a quick nap, have milk in a plate at the Dianahof, drink a quick curdled milk at the Maxtal, dine at the Neptun (vegetable omelette, Emmenthal, a portion of raw eggs and a portion of fresh peas), then sit on a bench in the municipal park to count your money, visit the pastry shop, and then sleep as much in one night as I was able to sleep in all the twenty-one that I spent here."

The forest air has stimulated his appetite. Franz bankrupts himself buying good lunches, strolls along eating juicy black cherries. He has put on weight, is writing, walks for hours in the woods. Bare-chested, he lies down full length in ditches lined with warm, thick grass. He stays there, alone, in the sun, sheltered from view. Such happiness! This landscape of low hills is his favorite landscape, the sea and mountains are too heroic for him.

He learns from Max that his Hebrew professor, Georg Langer, is in Marienbad with a distinguished personage, the Rabbi of Belz, one of the leaders of Hasidism. Out of curiosity, and to please Max, he joins the dozen people escorting the sainted man on one of his evening strolls. The next day, he sends Max a long account of the actions and gestures of the rabbi, an enigmatic man who rarely spoke.

Once back in Prague, the prospect of marriage awakens his anxieties all over again. He says to himself: We feel close to each other, we think we grasp each other solidly, whereas we are grasping the wind.

In his letters to Felice over the next four months, he talks about nothing but the Jewish People's Home, where she has agreed to volunteer. His tone is despotic, he expects a kind of submission or obedience from her. He is savoring, he says, the happiness of commanding another human being.

He requests photographs of his fiancée surrounded by all the little girls she is teaching: "The photographs show many traits that one would never see with one's own eyes," he tells her.

He gives her advice on every aspect of these young refugees from Eastern Europe, whose lives fascinate him down to the smallest detail. He sends them books almost daily, comments on every volume, heaps praise on Dickens's *Little Dorrit*, and tops off his packages with candies, chocolate, cocoa, and games.

He even writes her: "It's a little as though these girls were my children. The Home brings us so close together, creates such a strong spiritual link between us, that I want to pay for any expenses you incur on behalf of these children. Give them your help."

His only other topic of conversation is the Goltz Gallery in Munich, which organizes evenings of modern literature and has invited Max Brod and Kafka to read from their works. Max decides to read poems, and Franz will read "In the Penal Colony," which he believes to be the best thing he wrote in 1914.

He suggests to Felice that she join him in Munich. He doesn't yet know the date of the reading, he is not even sure it will take place. But he keeps returning to the subject of the trip. It will take place—no, there will be no trip. I'll go—no, I won't have obtained the visa nor the necessary permission from the censorship bureau.

"Miracle upon miracle," everything falls into place. Felice gives an excuse why she can't go. He insists. She gives in. He leaves Prague alone on Friday, November 10, very early in the morning. Max is staying behind. The Post Office Bureau, where he has a high-ranking job, has refused to allow him two days off. He assigns Franz the task of reading his poems.[9]

Franz arrives in Munich late in the afternoon. Felice is waiting for him at the Hotel Bayerischer Hof. That night at eight o'clock, Franz reads his "sordid story" without the slightest emotion, he says, as though the text meant nothing to him, his mouth colder than the mouth of an empty stove.[10] Whereas in general, he warms up to the point of frenzy. His friends still remember his reading of "The Metamorphosis" as energized and intoxicating.

The reading at Munich is a staggering failure. Felice, like most of the other listeners, is horrified at the

---

9 Kafka was irritated to discover that the Goltz Gallery had invited him only at Max Brod's request, and he was determined to give his friend a portion of the honorarium he received for his double performance.

10 Rilke did not attend this reading, as some have believed, but after reading "The Metamorphosis" he wrote to Kafka's editor: "Please keep for me anything published by FK. I am not, as I may promise you, his worst reader."

cruelty of the punishments inflicted on the inmates of the penitentiary, where everyone is guilty, where there is no other penalty than death, where suffering never leads to redemption.

The next day, a Saturday, at lunchtime, they enter an abominable pastry shop. Felice, angry, tells him abruptly what she thinks of his text, and the devil take the hindmost. Her hostility wounds him deeply. In lively tones he tells her: "My sense of guilt is always strong enough, you don't need to excite it further. But I am not strong enough to take such abuse. And this is not the only one of my texts to be painful. Everything I have written up to now is also like that. Our times, and mine in particular, are extremely painful. Mine for longer than anyone else's. God knows to what depths I would have descended if I had been allowed to write as much as I wanted!"

"Thank God you've been kept from it! No one needs to hear such atrocities."

"Atrocities are everywhere, even at our door. I sent you Arnold Zweig's book, *Ritual Murder in Hungary*. Did you read it? I burst into tears at certain passages. I had to put it down."

"Your penal colony is even more disgusting than that Jewish tragedy! The harrow that carves the law into a prisoner's flesh, what sadism! How could you!"

"The Law cannot be taught, it must be absorbed into one's blood. But you haven't liked anything I've written. Not one of my collections has met your approval. Not even *Meditation*, whose royalties—with your consent—are paid to you."

"That has nothing to do with it! And you're the one, I shouldn't have to remind you, who wanted it that way. I never asked you for anything. And let's talk, why don't we, about the sums your publisher sends me!"

Building to a pitch of irritation, she reproaches him for having made her come to Munich: "I wanted to see you in Berlin. But once again, you only thought of yourself, of your own pleasure, not mine. I'm getting to know just how selfish you are."

"I can't accept the fact that you—you in particular—reproach me for selfishness, and that you do it so lightly, as though it were the most obvious thing."

He leaves at dawn on Sunday.

While their first separation had blocked his creative energy, the disaster and the argument in Munich trigger an extraordinary spate of productivity. Other than the fourteen stories that compose *A Country Doctor*, he also writes "The Bridge," "The Hunter Gracchus," "Astride the Coal

Scuttle," "The Great Wall of China," "The Neighbor," "An Everyday Incident," "The Truth About Sancho Panza," "The Silence of the Sirens," and "Reflections on Sin."

He has never worked so well or in such agreeable conditions. During the day, he lives in the lovely little house lent to him by Ottla on Alchemists Street. It's wonderful to live there, and wonderful to walk home around midnight to sleep in the apartment he rents at the Schönborn Palace, a handsome structure on Mala Strana with two beautiful high-ceilinged rooms, red and gold; he could be living in Versailles. He describes it to Felice at length at the beginning of January.[11]

In July, the Kafka family celebrates the pair's second engagement, less sumptuously than the first, the war has been raging for three years. The day after the ceremony, the engaged couple leave for Arad, in Transylvania, where one of Felice's sisters lives. The two stop over for a day or two in Budapest, the trip is long, not very restful, and their relationship is up and down.

He returns to Prague alone after a brief stay in Vienna.

He sleeps a little better.

The wedding is set for September.

---

11 Between this letter dated early January and another dated September 30, 1917, no letters have survived. A black hole of nine months.

Freedom . . . Freedom!

He doesn't know exactly when during the night it started. He tells Ottla four o'clock in the morning, and Felice five o'clock. He was sleeping and a strange sensation wakes him, a flow of saliva in his mouth, an unusual taste. He sits up, spits it out. And then he lights his lamp to see what he has vomited up. Odd, it's a clot of blood, bright red and glistening. Excited as one always is by something new, at the same time frightened, he gets up. Immediately he spits up a second clot. Then a third, then a thin, continuous trickle of blood. He paces back and forth in his room, goes to the window, opens it wide, looks outside, breathes in the warm air, dawn is a long way off. He looks distractedly at his watch, walks back toward his bed. More blood keeps coming. He drinks a little water, rinses his mouth to clear it of the unpleasant taste. He stares at the towel soaked with blood, which has now turned to a dark, almost black, shade of red. He tells himself he has just lost the battle that he has waged for the last five years, he is not Napoleon, he will not emerge from Corsica. His headaches and insomnia have worn him out. It is a crushing defeat, an unconditional capitulation, which he signs with his blood.

Behind this sense of failure, behind this bitterness, he feels excitement mounting in him, an exhilarating sense of freedom. The battle is over. It is the end of five years of torment, the end of the headaches, the end of the insomnia, that have driven him crazy. From the rubble arises a wonderful sensation of freedom, a sudden lightness. He soars, at peace with himself. He goes back to bed, sleeps until morning.

He has never slept better.

The next day, the blood starts up again, less abundantly. He decides to say nothing to his parents. He goes to his doctor, Dr. Mühlstein, who diagnoses an acute bronchitis.

"A chest cold in August, when I have never had any sort of cold even in the depths of winter?" says Franz skeptically.

That same night, and the following days, more blood. The doctor orders tests and a chest X-ray. At Max's urging, Franz consults a specialist, Professor Pick, on September 4: "The upper portions of both lungs are infected, and there is a risk of tuberculosis. You need to take a long cure in the countryside, with a great deal of rest, light, fresh air, and sun."

To the doctor's surprise, Franz shakes his hand and thanks him warmly. *Very well!*

He bounds wildly down the staircase from the third-floor office and runs to tell Max the news.

Max is thunderstruck. "There is a risk of tuberculosis? You don't seem to realize how serious this could be."

"Illness can be a tutelary angel, only its progress is diabolical. For the moment, the blow I have just received feels like something wonderful. There is a great deal of sweetness in being ill."

"I don't understand. Does this disaster make you happy?"

"You shouldn't say it in that tone. It's not as simple as all that. But three months in the country, in sunlight, far from the office. Such freedom!"

He adds: "I am not going to keep my illness a secret, but I don't want to say anything about it to my parents. They have enough to worry about. Be careful around them."

On September 9, three months after spitting up blood, he writes to Felice. He tells her the reason for his silence: a pulmonary hemorrhage, suffered at the age of thirty-four with no prior warning or family precedent. He goes on to say that he has tuberculosis, but that the headaches and insomnia—his worst sufferings—have stopped tormenting him. In typical fashion, he makes a joke of it: "The brain said, Things can't go on like this, and after five years the lungs decided to do something about it." He adds: "I behave toward tuberculosis like a child clinging to its mother's skirts."

He further informs her that he is going for a rest cure to his sister's farm in Zürau. Ottla is an angel who carries him on her wings through a world full of hazards. In this farewell letter, which he starts "Dearest" as usual, he shows no trace of self-pity. He is drawing up a report for his "poor, dear Felice," a report that sounds the knell to their singular love affair.

He arrives in Zürau on the night of September 12, 1917. Other than two brief returns to Prague for further

X-rays and a doctor's visit, he doesn't budge from there. "On no account do I wish to leave Zürau," he writes Max, "I hang on to it with clenched teeth." He will stay there until April 30, 1918. Seven months, the most peaceful in his life.

When he arrives at his sister's, she is just putting the last of the hop harvest into the barn. Her brother-in-law, Karl Hermann, is fighting at the front, and she is running his farm, with the help of a farm manager.

There are several photographs of Franz and Ottla standing in front of the farmhouse, a squat, welcoming structure in a wooded, hilly landscape. Franz's room, though it faces northeast, is perfect, spacious, warm. His only complaint is the noise: a tinsmith starts to hammer on his tin at dawn, and if he stops for a moment it is only to let a worker take his turn pounding on wood. From the barnyard across the way come all the animal sounds of Noah's ark, the geese run shrieking to the pond like furies, and the mice make an inordinate noise in the attic. In a nearby house is the only piano in all northwest Bohemia, belonging to a rich farmer's daughter who presses fiercely on the pedal while dreaming of a life in Prague.

Franz is no longer looking for peace and quiet in this life. The pure air, the forest, and the light are enough for him. He has found a spectacular spot in which to stretch out in the sun: it is on a height, or rather on a small plateau in the center of a vast semicircular basin. Bare-chested or in his underwear, he lies there looking out like a king, on a huge old armchair with two footstools in front of him. He is almost entirely hidden from view. From time to time, though rarely, a head or two may pop up above the edge of the plateau and shout, "Come down off your bench!"

He doesn't move. For hours at a time he sits motionless in the sun, drinks liters and liters of raw milk, as his doctor ordered, either chilled or very hot.

"Perhaps," he says to Ottla, "I will become the village idiot some day."

He joins in the farmwork a little. He feeds the goats, which consists of bending down the leafiest branches of a bush until the goats can reach them. He watches the animals as they noisily crunch their meal. They look like Polish Jews, this one like his Uncle Alfred, that one like Felix, that other like Ernst.

At night, in the kitchen, he sits and peels vegetables. He takes the trouble to send a pair of partridges and four kilos of flour to Max and Oscar. Even in farm country, it's hard to find meat or butter at this point. Eggs are scarce too.

He rereads *David Copperfield*, to which "The Stoker," the first chapter of his American novel, owes so much, as he freely admits. He dreams of his father, of the battle of

Tagliamento, which was fought the previous month, of Franz Werfel. He writes letters to his parents, his friends, and to Max, who is facing a marital crisis.

He composes a letter breaking off his relationship with Felice but decides it is even more equivocal than his feelings and does not send it.

He observes the peasants whom he sees around him: "They are nobles who have found refuge in agriculture, they have organized their work with such wisdom and humility that they are protected from all upheavals, true citizens of the earth."

His illness? He is hardly aware of it. He has no fever, hardly coughs, admittedly sweats and is short of breath, but he has gained some weight back and he is sleeping better. His sister is glad to have him around. When he sees her at nightfall coming toward him with a blanket or a bowl of hot broth, he says: "We make an ideal couple. I've never felt so well as living alone with you."

Felice announces her intention to visit. Franz tries to talk her out of it, such a long journey, so many transfers from train to train . . . She insists. All right, then let her come! She arrives on September 21 after a trip lasting thirty hours. Weariness and emotional distress are stamped on her face. Her presence awakens nothing in him but guilt. He looks at her, surprised at feeling no emotion except anxiety at having his routine disrupted. He finds nothing to say to her, relying on Ottla to keep the conversation going and lead Felice on a tour. That evening, under his sister's gaze and solely to be agreeable to everyone, he manages to play his part, he hasn't lost his talents as an actor. Felice relaxes, perhaps even starts to hope again. Franz seems in such good health!

She leaves the next day in the late afternoon. He watches her climb into a carriage with Ottla and start off around the pond. He takes a straight line and finds himself once more in front of the woman he has pursued with his love for five years. Today, his face impassive, he waves at her listlessly. Farewell!

The following Sunday, he goes to the train station to meet his mother, who has come down for the day. She is unaware of her son's illness, delighted only to know that he is resting at Ottla's, in the countryside, far from the horrors of war. Stepping off the train, she exclaims, "My, how healthy you look!"

Seeing him smile, she adds that two or three days before she asked Felice whether her son was in a better mood: "And do you know what she answered? That she hadn't noticed!"

He avoids looking directly at his mother, who has never had the time to think of herself. She is puffy and distended from her six confinements, a lifetime of toil, and a total lack of care. He thinks of his oldest sister, a slender young woman just three or four years ago, who now, after giving birth to two children, has a swollen body that is already starting to look like his mother's. He feels so much distress on their account that he wants to avoid burdening them with his illness. As far as his family is concerned, he is resting. Nothing more.

Hermann Kafka is not so easily fooled. He asks Ottla repeatedly: "Why is your brother extending his vacation week after week? Just because he is tired? It doesn't seem possible."

On a visit to Prague on November 22, Ottla takes advantage of her mother's being busy in the kitchen to tell her father briefly about Franz. The mention of tuberculosis makes a strong impression on him, he says nothing to his daughter but his face registers a change of expression.

She reassures him: "In Zürau, Franz is putting on weight, he is sleeping well, he has everything he needs. Freed from the office and the factory, he is a different man. He is going to recover, ask his doctor, you'll see!"

Her father remains concerned.

"Don't say anything to Mother, or to my sisters," adds Ottla. "Franz asks you not to."

After receiving visits from Felice, his mother, and his secretary, Fräulein Kaiser, all highly agitating, Franz is loath to have Max, Oscar, or Felix come to visit. He no longer feels in any condition to see them, he prefers writing. He tells them about his "night of mice." "What a race they are, mute, noisy, horrid. The clandestine work of an oppressed proletarian race that rules at night. I didn't dare get up and light the lamp yesterday. All I could manage was to shout a few times to frighten them. In the morning, sad and disgusted, I couldn't get out of bed. I lay there listening to the sound of one tireless mouse working in the cupboard, either finishing last night's work or getting a start on tonight's. Now I've brought the cat into my room, the cat I've always secretly hated. Even the warm smell and good taste of the home-baked bread is tinged with mouse."

He tries to create a void around and within him, as the Taoists prescribe.

"I am a Chinese man," he says to his sister.[12]

Stretched out on the newly arrived deck chair, a blanket over his legs, he looks out at the hills. The forests, in their late autumn colors, glow in the evening light as though on fire.

The voices of the world fall silent, or become scarce.

---

12 According to Elias Canetti, Kafka is the only typically Chinese writer to be found in the West.

"It Wasn't to Be Your Destiny"[13]

In Zürau, in front of Ottla, Felice didn't dare to question Franz closely, and he parried her attempts to talk to him privately. Riding the train home, she doesn't know what to think. Franz is in good health, he coughs only at night and not that much. Why was he so distant, cold, and uncommunicative? Before her departure, they stood for a fairly long time on the doorsill looking at the village square. They hardly spoke, she was unhappy about

---

13 The consolation that Julia Kafka offered her son, on learning that his second engagement had been called off.

the senseless trip and Franz's strange behavior. Was it possible he had forgotten about Marienbad? Forgotten that he was writing her barely a few weeks back, "You are a part of me"?

Back in Berlin, she waits for his letter. The days go by, nothing comes. Her bridal trousseau, arranged in neat piles around her room, seems to taunt her. Her mother's gaze bristles with reproach. Her aunts, her friends, and her colleagues are continually asking, "So when is the wedding?"

Uncertainty taints even her simplest pleasures. She must see Franz alone, face to face as at Marienbad, demand an explanation, even if it's to be the last. Though her Christmas vacation may have to be sacrificed, she must get to the bottom of the whole thing.

She asks Franz in a pleading letter to meet her in Prague.

"You can't hide away any longer. You owe me the truth, the whole truth."

He leaves Zürau on December 24. On December 25, Felice is in Prague. Their first day together goes well, they discuss every subject but the main one. Felice is calm, affectionate. That night they go and visit Max. Neither Franz nor Felice manages to join the general conversation. Struck dumb for the entire evening, they both seem at a loss. The next morning, Franz rings Max's doorbell at 7:30. Spend the morning with me, he says. They meet up at the Café de Paris.

After a long moment of silence, Max asks, "What do you want from me?"

"Nothing."

"Then why did you ask me to spend the morning with you?"

"To help me kill time. I have made my decision and it is unshakable. What I have to do, I can only do alone. I am convinced that in breaking off my engagement, this time once and for all, I am doing the right thing. I don't doubt it for a second, or I could never do it. But putting an end to five years of love, however right it may be, is still a great injustice. What remains an enigma to me is Marienbad. Why . . ."

He doesn't finish his sentence.

That afternoon and the following day are terrible. He has to convince Felice that she cannot become attached to a man like him. He accuses himself of ruining her life, he has made her fall out with Grete Bloch, he has made her fall out with her sister Erna, he has contributed to the death of her father, he has tortured her in every way conceivable, he has tyrannized her, he has insisted that she learn to swim, that she perform gymnastics, that she stop eating sugar cubes, that she volunteer ever longer hours at the Jewish People's Home . . .

Felice puts her hand over his mouth: "Stop, Franz, please, you are talking nonsense, absolute nonsense."

"Then stop asking me why I am putting an end to it, don't prolong my humiliation."

More gently, he continues: "I'll tell you a secret, I am not going to recover my health. My tuberculosis is not an illness that you put to rest on a deck chair, it is a weapon that I need, one that will stay with me as long as I live. And we cannot both remain alive, my illness and I."

On the morning of December 27, he accompanies Felice to the train station. He knows that he will never see her, never hear from her again. He watches her climb into a carriage, watches the train pull away, he cannot contain the emotions working in him. Pale, his face hard and cold, he seeks out Max. His friend is at the office, and he is not alone. One of his colleagues sits at an adjoining desk. Paying no attention to this man, whom he seems not to see, paying no attention to the bustle going on around them, Franz sits down next to his friend. He bursts into tears.

Max is worried, it is the first time since he has known Franz that he has ever seen him cry, cry openly, the tears rolling down his cheeks. Between sobs, he hears him say: "Isn't it terrible that it should come to this, isn't it terrible?"

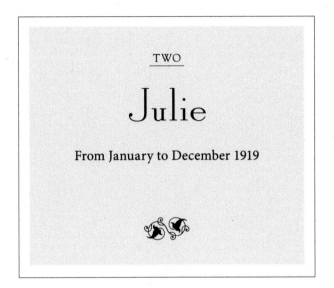

TWO

Julie

From January to December 1919

"One has simply been sent out as a biblical dove, and having found nothing green, now slips back into the darkness of the ark."

—LETTER TO MILENA

Julie, the Forgetting

S panish influenza, rampant across Europe, strikes
him in early October. His temperature soars to 105
degrees Fahrenheit and remains there. His mother
tends to him day and night, thinks he will die, cries at his
bedside. She remembers her two sons Georg and Heinrich, who died at the ages of six and eighteen months.

Franz recovers, then relapses. His lungs deteriorate.
When he gets over the flu, he is so weakened that his
doctor prescribes a long rest cure in the countryside.

On November 30, 1918, his mother drops him off in
Schelesen, a village north of Prague that Franz knows. At

this time of year, he is the only guest at the small hotel kept by Fräulein Olga Studl. He stays there four months, at sixty krone a day.

He spends the days lying in a deck chair on his balcony, breathing the fresh air, swathed in blankets, looking out at the wooded hills. The quiet is broken only at lunchtime by the snarling of the hotel's dogs, Meta and Rolf, fighting over the remains of Franz's meal, which he tosses out the window to them.

One day in January, a second guest arrives. It is a young woman of twenty-eight, Julie Wohryzek. Winter is at its height, and the hotel, the hills, the forests are buried in crystalline snow, which sparkles as far as the eye can see. It could be Lapland, and there is no traveling except by horse-drawn troika. But the intense cold outdoors keeps the two convalescents prisoners inside "this truly enchanted habitation."

The early moments of their relationship belong in a film comedy. Franz and Julie keep walking into each other, as they traverse the hotel's deserted hallways, or enter the empty dining room, or rise from their respective tables, which are yards apart, or when they sit down in the cavernous drawing room. It becomes so funny that as soon as they see each other, they break out laughing. They laugh about their strange resemblance, about having the same shape of face, the same mouth, they laugh about their shyness, they laugh for no reason, and without stopping, they look at each other and can't hold back the laughter that wells up and leaves them in confusion. Whenever they start giggling, Fräulein Olga Studl raises her hands to the heavens and mutters, "Those two, those two . . . what on earth is going on?"

They spend six weeks together. At night they hold long conversations. He tells her about his doubly failed engagement. She is just getting over the death of her fiancé, killed at the front. He finds Julie common and surprising, pretty (she reminds him of Grete Bloch), honest, likable, and shy. "She is a fragile counter girl," he writes Max, "deeply ignorant and full of resignation." He adds, somewhat cynically: "She is no less insignificant than this housefly, for example, flying toward the light."

Franz's eccentricities surprise Julie. He spends his nights writing to his friends, his sister, his parents. He rises at noon, eats only vegetables and dried fruits, drinks liters of milk. At night, he reads aloud for hours on end, pacing back and forth, gesticulating like an actor, his eyes shining with pleasure. He intrigues her with his insatiable curiosity, questioning her tirelessly about her work as a milliner. How does she go about creating a hat? Does she start from a sketch or from a piece of fabric? How long does it take to make one? Do her hats have veils? Flowers? Whom does she sell them to, and for how much?

With a tact that she appreciates, he also takes an interest in her father's work as a shoemaker and a synagogue watchman in a poor hamlet. The number of Yiddish expressions that stud her speech, some of them quite shocking, disconcerts him, but he hides the fact.

They both feel that, despite their social and cultural differences, they are intimately suited to each other. They spend more and more time together. In the middle of the night, wrapped in a blanket, Franz walks the length of the hallway leading to Julie's room to slip a letter under her door. Once back in bed, he waits for the reply. When they greet each other, morning and night, he takes the risk of holding the young woman's hand a little longer than normal. Soon, he is discussing marriage: "It is the highest goal, but it is not for me. My health is too poor."

"Although my reasons are different, I am no longer interested in marriage either," she says.

"Don't you want to have children?"

"No, ever since the war and the death of my fiancé, I really don't."

"What kind of life do you want to live?"

"A life that would help me forget the misery I've known. All I dream about is the movies, the comic opera, fashion. Nothing else."

"As we have both opted against marriage, we cannot stay together. The court of public opinion obliges us to separate."

For several days, they bravely resist their mutual attraction. They avoid each other, take lunch and dinner at different times. Julie cuts short her evenings in the drawing room. Franz lingers longer in his bedroom. They must avoid each other or they would start using the familiar *Du* and fall into each other's arms.

The time has come to part. A melancholy moment. Julie has asked one of her sisters to accompany her back to Prague. Franz catches only a glimpse of this woman, who seems a little disoriented but a thoroughly good person.

He remains alone at Schelesen for another three weeks, until the end of March. He doesn't write Julie, not even a word. But now that she is gone, he is obsessed with her. He's convinced that things can't just be left as they are.

Shortly after his return to Prague, the two arrange to meet—how could it have been otherwise? They become lovers.

This was to be the start of a peaceful, happy period. They meet almost every day, but, in order not to be seen together, they take long walks in the forest, along the dark alleys of the Riegerpark, or after nightfall in the streets of Prague. They hide from others, and this cautiousness is humiliating to Franz.

When his sister Ottla becomes officially engaged and sets the date of her wedding for July 15,[14] the fear of winding up alone makes him do something crazy: he proposes to Julie. She refuses. He insists, lays out arguments, wears away at the young woman's resistance. He persuades himself that it would be a marriage of love and a rational one as well. Julie provides him the sense of safety that he needs.

He again combs Prague for an apartment, neighborhood by neighborhood.

One night he announces the news of his engagement to his parents. He wants to introduce them to his new fiancée.

---

14 Ottla, over the opposition of her parents, married Josef David, a Christian Czech. While Max Brod saw the marriage as a loss for Judaism, Kafka supported his sister: "You are doing something extraordinary, and to do something extraordinary correctly is extraordinarily difficult. But if you manage never to forget the responsibility that such a difficult act entails, you will do more than if you had married ten Jews."

"A shoemaker's daughter?" says Hermann. "A woman whose father is the poorest man in all Bohemia? That's who Herr My Son wants to marry? A revolting goose who snares you in a moment? Your sister is marrying a Catholic, but you have just dealt me an even more painful blow. You are trying to kill me, is that what you want?"

Hermann threatens to go into exile to avoid the dishonor of such a mismatch. He reminds his son that his engagement to Felice was twice broken off, that enormous sums were spent on his behalf for nothing, and that six months of rent went down the drain! Two failures are not enough for Herr My Son, now he must have a third? If you need a whore, go to the bordello. And if you can't manage to do that alone at your age, I'll take you there myself.

For the first time, Franz doesn't let himself be terrorized. The torrent of insults and contempt from his father only reinforces his decision. The day he finds an apartment, a shabbily furnished one-bedroom on the outskirts of Prague, he sets a date for the wedding.

He arranges for the publication of the banns.

On Monday, Julie and he visit the apartment. They are sitting on the couch, huddled together. The young woman savors the moment. She has won this home after untold suffering. At her side is her husband-to-be, the promise of happiness. Tears of joy run down her face. Franz is also shaken. He has just realized how close he is to disaster. On Sunday, he will move in, live day after day with Julie, her dresses, her hats, and her underwear, her smells and her fripperies, her voice chattering away in this dingy, dark, overcrowded cell. He will stop writing. His heart thumps. His vision blurs. The walls, the ceiling, and the floor start to spin, his face, his body break out in sweat. He feels on the point of collapse.

On Friday, two days before the wedding, the landlord changes his mind. The apartment is no longer available.

He is saved.

For several weeks, Franz pretends that life is continuing as before. He walks with Julie in the Riegerpark, the botanical garden. They have lunch together often, swim together at Cernosic.

Finally he can't go on, can't ignore the warning signals drumming in his head. His insomnia is driving him crazy, he compares himself to a man burning alive. He offers Julie a pact of friendship and faith: "Let's go on seeing each other as often as you like, but let's discard the idea of marriage."

In mid-November, unable to stand it any longer, he runs away. Where to? To Schelesen, where they met. Max accompanies him. Over a period of ten days, Franz composes the "Letter to His Father."

When he returns to Prague, he shows it to Ottla, then gives it to his mother, who wisely refuses to pass it on to its intended recipient. Hermann Kafka would go to his grave unaware of the eighty-page letter his son wrote to him in the days following his aborted engagement to Julie. Hermann Kafka would never hear the reproaches his son leveled at him, and those he leveled at his son. Franz, typically enough for a lawyer, advocated for both parties. He prosecuted a double suit: the son's lawsuit against the father and the father's stinging rebuttal of his son.

Was it for his father that Franz intended this settling of accounts and this peace offering? It seems unlikely. Franz knew perfectly well (how often he complained of it!) that his father never opened any of his books, even *A Country Doctor*, which was dedicated to him. Hermann never read a page of it, not a single word. Every time Franz gave him a collection of his works, his father, without looking at it, without touching it, as though it were a disgusting thing, would utter this sentence, which became a family catchphrase: "Put it on my night stand."

Franz knew what the fate of his letter would be in his father's hands. Which explains, perhaps, why he spoke with such extraordinary freedom. Did it work as he had hoped it would? Did he approach close enough to the truth to make his life, his death, a little easier?

On his return from Schelesen, he starts seeing Julie again, but nothing is the same. He is distracted, abrupt, silent, shuttered. The days pass in boredom, idleness, silence, anxiety. The affair is treading water. But not for long.

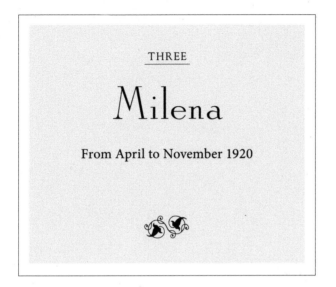

THREE

Milena

From April to November 1920

"*I'm the most Western Jewish of them all. In other words, to exaggerate, not one second of calm has been granted me, nothing has been granted me, everything must be earned, not only the present and future, but the past as well—something that is perhaps given every human being—this too must be earned, and this probably entails the hardest work of all. If the Earth turns to the right—I'm not sure it does—then I would have to turn to the left to make up for the past. But as it is I don't have the least bit of strength for these obligations; I can't carry the world on my shoulders—I can barely carry my winter coat.*"

—LETTER TO MILENA

Milena, the End of an Illusion

They meet at the Café Arco. Franz has gone there to buy himself the thing he loves most: a cup of hot chocolate under a mountain of cream. He is sitting at a table alone. She comes toward him: "Dr. Kafka? I'm Milena Jesenská, wife of Ernst Polak. You know him, I believe?"

She points toward her husband, who is talking to a large redheaded woman. Franz rises immediately to his feet, bows to the very young lady with the lovely blue eyes standing in front of him. Slender and blond, she looks squarely at him and smiles at his awkwardness. He has knocked over the sugar bowl without noticing it.

He stares at her, forgetting to answer her question.

"I'd like to translate several of your books into Czech: *The Stoker, The Judgment, The Metamorphosis*, and *In the Penal Colony*."

"All that trouble? You shouldn't."

"Of course I should. Your books are the most important of the new crop of German literature. I've already translated *The Stoker*, and your editor, Kurt Wolff, has asked me to obtain your permission."

"You're a translator?"

"Yes, I just said that. And a journalist. May I send you the text for corrections?"

"Do you live in Prague?"

"No, in Vienna."

They trade addresses. She waves good-bye, he watches her walk away.

He remembers the clothes she was wearing that day, her lively hands, her frail figure between the tables of the Café Arco. Yes, he still remembers that.

He leaves Prague in early April. He is going to Meran in the South Tirol for a rest. He is constantly weary. He repeatedly requests time off from work and can't seem to end his affair with Julie. She clings to him and cries. Does he hope that being away for two months will put an end to her obstinacy? He has said nothing to her about the meeting at the Café Arco or the two letters he has received from Milena, two letters that are never out of his pocket and that he fingers like a talisman.

In Meran he settles into the Ottoburg Pension, run by Fräulein Fröhlich. From his balcony he sees climbing flowers at the height of his room and exuberant tropical vegetation in the garden below. A sparrow visits him at breakfast time. Franz tosses it a few breadcrumbs and watches the reaction. The bird stands in the sunlight on the balcony. It covets the life-giving food, the crumbs that lie in shadow on the threshold to Franz's room. A few little hops and the bird could gobble them all down. But it is afraid to venture into unknown territory. It tentatively makes a few jumps forward, stops, advances a little farther, hops away, fluffs out its feathers to give itself courage. Desire propelling it, the sparrow jumps and lands a few centimeters from the feast. Then it retreats. It flies away, ruled by fear.

Toward mid-April, Franz starts to write Milena. He is no longer the dashing seducer who, on the night of August 13, 1912, rang at Max Brod's door and decided, there and then, to win Felice. He is now thirty-nine years old, his hair has turned gray, he no longer takes the stairs four at a time. He spends most of his waking hours in a deck chair. He is easily winded from walking.

When he meets Milena, the woman he had never hoped to meet, especially now, especially so late, he knows his time is limited. This is no longer the season for pleasantries.

And Milena is not Felice.

She is only twenty-three when she enters his life like a hurricane. Twenty-three, but she already has an eventful past and a scandalous reputation. As a child she took care of her mother for months. She saw her suffer, waste away, and die in her arms. Her father, a famous stomatologist and a stiff, brutal man, refused to care for his wife himself.

Neglected and bereaved of her mother, the adolescent experimented with cocaine and ran with a fast crowd. One night she swam across the Moldau River fully dressed to meet a lover. She spent her afternoons in cafes, posed naked for painters, rented hotel rooms in which to meet her two closest friends, Staša and Jarmila (there was whispered talk of sapphic love). She offered them armfuls of flowers, dresses, ornaments. Money burned her fingers.

She was eighteen and attending a concert when she met Ernst Polak and decided to live with him. The young man was a womanizer, a gambler, and a night creature with a vague connection to writing. When Dr. Jesensky learned of his daughter's attachment to a Jew and a cafe-table writer, he had her locked up in a psychiatric clinic outside Prague. She lived with the insane for nine months, obtained her release on reaching adulthood, and raced off to marry Polak. Dr. Jesensky cut off all ties to his daughter.

The two moved to Vienna. Now money is scarce and life hard. Milena writes columns for magazines and newspapers in Prague, brilliant columns that are avidly read by feminists. She teaches Czech, translates foreign novels. Days when she has no money, when she has nothing to eat but apples and tea, she puts on an old cap and walks to the main train station, where she hauls luggage for travelers. Her husband, "the man with forty mistresses," openly cheats on her. Often the worse for drink, he mistreats Milena and runs up debts that she scrambles to repay. When she meets Kafka, her health is dicey, she has a recurring case of bronchitis, she has coughed up blood two or three times, her marriage is falling apart, and she has no money.

Franz and Milena begin writing each other in April, and they stop in November. Less than eight months. He writes to her in German, she answers in Czech, usually in pencil. A subject for complaint. Of his letters, about 150 survive. None of Milena's.[15] All that remains of hers are her articles—tributes to the little black dress, to fashion, to cafes, to the popular quarters on Sundays, to trains, to a film by Charlie Chaplin; a brilliant satire of marriage and communal life, "The Devil at the Hearth"; and the eight feverish, impassioned letters that she wrote to Max as her affair with the man she still called "Frank" was coming to an end. In his early letters to her, Franz appended his second initial to his first name. Milena never noticed the z. And he never corrected her. For her alone he was a different person.

Milena confides about what is going poorly in her life: her health. He becomes alarmed, begs her to leave Vienna and find rest by a lake, perhaps in Meran, where he is staying.

"My God! Milena, if you were here!" he writes. "But I would be lying if I said that I missed you: for by the most cruel and perfect magic, you are here, even as I am, no, even more than I am. This is not a joke, I actually find myself thinking that you must miss me here, since you are very much here but asking yourself: Where is he? Didn't he write that he was in Meran?"

---

15 After Kafka's death, she asked Max Brod to burn them.

She writes about her father and being cut off by him (Franz knows all about hard-hearted fathers, and on June 21 sends her his "Letter to His Father"), about her marital quarrels, her financial difficulties (he sends her money). In return, she asks him about his private life, his three engagements, his ties to Judaism, and his fears, all his fears.

From April to the end of June, they write each other every day, often several times a day, always by express mail. As they reach a feverish pitch, telegrams fly back and forth at a rapid rate. Franz addresses his letters to a fictional Frau Kramer, at the Poste Restante, where Milena goes to pick them up each morning and night. They both live in expectation, in impatient expectation, of learning more, and saying more: "This mania for letters is insane," Franz writes her. "One tilts one's head back, drinks the words down, knows nothing except that one doesn't want it to stop. Explain that to me, Professor Milena."

The attraction they feel for each other is so strong that by early June they are using the familiar *Du* and talking of love.

"Address me again with the word *Du*," he writes. "And look me in the eye."

Franz had often addressed the sturdy Felice as "My darling girl, my child." Today he calls Milena: "My baby, my baby." Yesterday he went so far as to call her "Mommy Milena." The impetuous young woman, whom Franz has described to Max as "a living fire, such as I have never seen before," summarily orders him never to use such ridiculous language again.

Reading Milena's calm letters to him, he is happy: "It is rain on my burning head." But when she castigates him, sends him goading messages (as she most often does), which are as inimical to him as holy water to the devil, he looks for a piece of furniture to crawl under and suffers wave after wave of anxiety.

"The letters, arising from incurable torment," he writes, "only cause incurable torment. The written kisses do not arrive at their destination, they are sipped by phantoms along the way."

By June 12, he can no longer stand the zigzagging of their letters.

"They have got to stop, Milena, they are driving us crazy. One no longer knows what one is writing, what the other is responding to, and, in any case, one trembles."

The following day he changes his mind: "Write to me every day just the same, two little lines, or one, or a single word, but if I do not get this single word I suffer inordinately."

When he writes that he is leaving Meran and returning to Prague, Milena asks him, begs him, to pass through Vienna. His letters are no longer enough. Franz takes fright, particularly as he has just received a telegram from Julie, which he can hardly bring himself to read: "Meeting in Karlsbad June 8, please confirm." He telephones his fiancée: I am too worn out to make the journey. And he is afraid, horribly afraid, of going to Vienna, of not measuring up to the illusion that his letters and his books have fostered.

"I don't want, I don't want (no, I am not stuttering), I don't want to pass through Vienna, the mental effort is more than I can bear, I have been ill since my three engagements. My headaches and all the old nights have turned my hair almost white. Consider that I am thirty-eight years old (double it, since I am Jewish), compared to your twenty-three Christian years."

"Come," she writes, "I am in such a funk, I need you actually here. I'm tired of looking at a face that is just a sheet of paper covered in words."

"I'm frightened. I'm not tired, but I'm frightened of the extraordinary fatigue that would result from the extraordinary nervous strain."

"Remember what you wrote me: 'And one time, and ten times, and a thousand times, and all the time I want to be near you.'"

"I was saying what I thought, Milena. But there are many things that escape me, and possibly everything es-capes me."

"Come, hold me in your arms. I love you."

"Every hour of my life to come looks at me and snickers: You received that letter, and you haven't been to Vienna? Haven't been to Vienna? Haven't been to Vienna? Haven't been to Vienna?"

"Come."

"I can't yet say whether I am coming to Vienna, but I'm fairly certain that I won't."

"You'll come."

"Today, I might say that I will surely come to Vienna. But tomorrow? I reserve my freedom."

"I'm expecting you."

"If I come to Vienna, I'll send a telegram on Tuesday or Wednesday."

"You'll come."

"Milena, if you don't receive an express letter on Thursday, it will mean that I have gone directly back to Prague. I have spent two nights without sleep."

"I want to see you."

"I'll be in Vienna on Tuesday, barring the unforeseen."

At ten a.m. on Tuesday, June 29, 1920, Franz arrives at the South Station. He drops his bags at the Hotel Riva ("Riva," a good omen), although there is a garage nearby with put-putting car engines. He sits down to a cup of hot chocolate and an assortment of cakes and composes a telegram: he tells Milena he has arrived in the city and sets a meeting for the next morning in front of his hotel at ten o'clock. His breakfast eaten, he drops the letter off at the Poste Restante, then tries to put the day to good use by visiting the sights, preparing for his meeting, and quieting his nerves. He is afraid that his presence, the sight of this long, thin person, will bring Milena to the ground with a thump, break the epistolary enchantment.

They spend four days together, from June 30 to July 4.

Four radiant days, to hear Milena tell it.

"If I close my eyes, I see you again in Vienna, near me, I see your white shirt and your suntanned neck, you were climbing the hill, your steps rang out behind me. You walked all day, you went up, you went down, you stayed in the sun, your head on my bare breast, you didn't cough once, you ate poorly, you were alert, gay, you slept all night." (How would she know? They never spent a night together.)

Franz is more reserved. True, he hasn't forgotten the forest where they took a long walk, the clearing where they lay on the warm grass, Milena's face above and then below his own, the sweetness of their physical contact, all too brief, and the fixing of their bodies' boundaries. He hasn't forgotten the wind that, on the way home, puffed out the sleeves of Milena's dress, Vienna on the horizon, the carriage ride through the popular quarters, the climb up the little paved street, the alleys in the evening light, and the happiness of lying on Milena's bare shoulder.

"How nice it is to be with you," he kept saying.

He often thinks of the wonderful stationery store they visited, where they stood pressed against one another. He is sorry he didn't stay there longer. He can still see the massive armoire in Milena's bedroom, he doesn't like that armoire, it reminds him of the one Felice bought, a funerary monument. All these young women, why do they need these gigantic pieces of furniture? What is to be buried there, once they are married?

Milena has mentioned Franz to her husband, and Ernst has sworn, in the style of a music-hall skit, that he will sock, no, strangle the hapless lover. Franz is still laughing about it. "If only he would do it!" he says to Milena.

He knows, even before leaving Vienna, that he is losing the battle. Each night he makes his way back to the Hotel Riva alone, and he spends his mornings alone. A bell rings in his ear: Milena isn't with you. She won't leave her husband for you. Your prayers will have no effect.

He thinks back to his meetings in Berlin with Felice. Every one of them was a disaster. Although his letters strengthened, tightened their relationship, his presence, like an acid, dissolved it. Was the same process happening here? he asks himself. On July 4, Milena rises at dawn and accompanies him to the station dressed in her prettiest dress, her good-bye dress. But when he kisses her on the platform (was it too public, too insistent?) the young woman recoils ever so slightly, and he knows that he has lost Milena. The novel they constructed together with so much passion, so many letters and letters and more letters, so many declarations and confessions, each offering his self, and her self, voluptuously to the other, is only a novel, a shimmering mirage on the horizon.

"I can't leave my husband for the moment."

It is the truth. The excuses Milena offers are weak: "Ernst is sick, he has no money, he can't live alone. And who will shine his boots?"

When he arrives back in Prague, Franz finds a letter on his desk from Julie, she asks to see him at three o'clock in front of her building. He decides to tell her everything. Arriving at six o'clock (he has sent word that he will be late), he notices that she looks quite unhealthy but is unmoved by it. Accustomed to speaking the truth, even to the smallest detail and whatever the consequences, he says, "I am with Milena, I am dissolved in Milena, I am only with Milena."

Done like an executioner.

Julie's face breaks apart, she trembles all over, she grows angry: "That woman already has a husband, and what's more a husband she loves. She goes behind his back to see you. You live in Prague, she lives in Vienna, and she needs you on top of everything? Let me write to her, she'll understand that I have only you. If I lose you, I have nothing, no reason to live."

"You'll still have my friendship and my affection, you know that perfectly well."

"I want to see what she's been writing you. Show me her letters."

"Out of the question."

"Give me her husband's address."

She begs him, driven by a bottomless despair. To appease her, and to bring the interview to a close, he gives her permission to write Milena.

It is after nightfall when they part. The next morning, Franz sends Julie an urgent message: "Don't send the letter to Vienna before we've talked about it."

Julie wrote the letter at dawn. She has just posted it when the telegram from Franz arrives. Panicked, she runs to the main post office. She is so relieved to intercept her letter that she gives all her money to the teller. That night, she turns the letter over to Franz.

Their meeting on that night is their last, they will never see each other again. Two rounds of letters follow in the days to come, then all between them is finished.

What does he do with Julie's pleading letter? He sends it, without breaking the seal, to Milena. And Milena answers the tearful girl.

What does Julie do with her rival's curt reply? She sends it to Franz without comment, only marking it up in pencil. She has double-underlined the sentence: "Forget all about him! He has never spoken a word to me about you, or so much as hinted at your existence in his letters."

A cruel lie! In his first letters to Milena, Franz mentioned Julie, whom he calls "the girl." He gave a faithful report of their engagement, their meetings, their talks, he even asked Milena to help him break off the relationship! He realizes how foolishly he has behaved only as his affair with Julie is coming to an end. He asks for forgiveness, but only from Milena.

We lose direct track of Julie after July 15, 1920, the day when, showing much good sense, she shows Franz the door. We know that she opened a millinery shop. Franz urges Ottla to visit it and buy a hat there.

A few years later, plagued by hallucinations, Julie is committed to the Weleslawin psychiatric asylum, the very institution Milena had been sent to by her father. There Julie dies. But in what year? 1930, 1931, 1932? Did she burn her fiancé's few letters to expel him from her life, as she had been expelled from his? None survives.

What we know about his relation with the pretty milliner, whom he describes as "almost an enchantress by nature," comes from the letter he wrote to her sister. This is the woman he glimpsed at Schelesen when she came to accompany Julie back to Prague. Why such a long account, some twenty pages, to a woman he didn't know and who wanted nothing from him? Someone, furthermore, who never spoke a word to him though she most certainly knew about her sister's romance and its termination. Was he trying to justify himself? Or leave a trace of the bond they shared, the events that drove them apart? Was it the impulse of a memoirist, intent on capturing the people he meets, the accidents of history, the bits of life?

Grete freed Franz from Felice, Milena got rid of "the girl" for him. Both did it in the same way, using weapons he had put in their hands: his letters.

After Vienna and the first crack in their relationship, Franz and Milena continue to write each other just as often as before, and just as lengthily. But Franz's tone is no longer the same. His love, obsessive as ever, brings him only suffering: "You, Milena, are what I love most, you are a part of me (even if I am never to see you again), but you are the knife with which I probe my wound."

His tone is sad, almost bitter, when he says: "Milena, don't let the memory of our four radiant days lead you into making a mistake. We owed many of our beautiful moments to your certainty of returning to your husband each night. I am no longer contesting him for possession of you. The battle is all happening inside you. Rather than freeing you from Ernst, I have strengthened your mutual ties."

And this: "If, during those four days, I had convinced you, you would no longer be in Vienna but in Prague."

"It's true, you asked me to leave Ernst and come with you. I didn't do it, I couldn't! I am too weak, too much a woman, to live the monastic life you lead, to take part in your strict asceticism. I have both feet on the ground, and a wretched love of life."

"The only way to save another person is through one's presence. There is no other way, Milena, and you know it."

"You're right. If I had gone with you when you were begging me not to abandon you, I would have given you proof of my love. This proof is something that you will always miss, and your fear will feed on it."

"My fear is the best thing about me, it makes up my substance, and perhaps it is also what you love in me."

In late July, Milena expresses a desire to meet without delay. There follows a tedious discussion about the date of the journey and its duration, one day or two? About the train schedules, "My head has turned into a railway station," he says. They choose to meet at the halfway point, on the border between Austria and Czechoslovakia. A few days before the departure, Milena falls sick. She cancels the trip. She admits to Franz that she hasn't found a plausible lie to tell her husband, whose violence she fears.

Then she decides that they will see each other on Sunday, August 14, for six hours, between two trains. By leaving Vienna at seven o'clock in the morning, she can reach Gmünd at eleven. She will return by a late-afternoon train and be back in Vienna that night. Her husband will never know of her escapade.

Gmünd is a disaster. Why? Neither of the lovers gives even the briefest account of it. Five or six times, Franz says to Milena: "The subject of Gmünd will have to be broached in our letters, or discussed between us."

But he never addresses it. Nor is Milena anxious to revisit what happened, or failed to happen, in Gmünd. A memory that neither party is interested in discussing, what is the point?

Other than the fact that they saw each other for six hours, what remains of this day? This brief and surprising exchange:

"Have you been unfaithful to me in Prague?"

"Milena, I don't even understand what the question could mean."

And this command from Franz: "Stop writing letters to Max. I don't want anyone to slip between us, or to influence us. If my state of health concerns you, I am the one who is sick. I alone can give you news of my health."

Indications suggest that in the border town of Gmünd, the two lovers (who are no longer lovers) talked at length, but as though they were strangers.

"Mostly," he writes Milena, "there were misunderstandings [about what?] and shame, a practically ineradicable shame [shame of what? Of his extreme tiredness, his impotence? Only desire is real, he had said], and lies ['if I had come to fetch you in Vienna, you would be by my side, the rest is lies']." Everything is his fault, he is so far below her: "Next to you, I feel dirty."

To take a step backward: What happened in the six weeks separating Vienna and Gmünd? In the multitude of details about this period there are perhaps elements of an answer.

The moment Franz leaves Vienna, his head empty, tired (another defeat!), the imperious and demanding Milena sends him a long list of errands. He runs from shop to shop in search of the knit jersey or the ten books that she has asked for. He stands in line for the export permit he must obtain for each of the packages, into which he slips a little money.

For two long days in a heat wave with the temperature at one hundred degrees Fahrenheit and the trams on strike, he wanders among the graves in the cemetery looking for the resting place of Jeníček, Milena's brother, who died as an infant. Franz's head spins from peering at headstone inscriptions whose gold has faded away. After a long and tedious search, he discovers that the baby was buried not under his father's name, Jesensky, but under his mother's. Milena had not mentioned this detail.

Does he ask himself as he lays a bunch of carnations on the edge of the stone why Milena sent him to the grave of this infant, dead more than twenty years? To punish him? For what? To mourn their love and the child he has not given her, will never give her?

She directs him to arrange a meeting with Laurin, the garrulous editor of the *Tribuna,* for which she writes. He must also make repeated visits to two of her childhood friends. The first of them he finds horrid: "Whenever I want to imagine hell," he says to Milena, "I think of Staša."

The other, Jarmila, looks like a specter, an angel of death. She is in the midst of a tragic story: her husband, Joseph Reiner, discovers that she has had a love affair (perhaps platonic) with one of his friends. He kills himself. The news of his suicide casts a shadow over Franz and Milena: What if Ernst should do the same?

A further, more difficult mission is to obtain a reconciliation with Milena's father. Milena is ill and short of funds, she would like her father to send her a regular allowance. Franz doesn't feel strong enough to confront haughty Professor Jesensky. Instead, he negotiates with the professor's assistant and mistress, Vlasta. After several rounds of back-and-forth, he obtains the desired result: Milena can take a rest cure by the lake at Saint-Gilgen as she had wanted.

When he gives her the news, she is indignant: "You've gone about it with such stupidity, such carelessness, such rotten clumsiness!"

He has spent six weeks running all over town in a heat wave, climbing endless spiral staircases, putting up with the babbling, the visits, and the thoughtless remarks of Staša and Jarmila, he has met for whole afternoons with people who revolted him and made him nervous. Drained of energy, he then spent his evenings in an armchair unable to move a muscle, his chest on fire, his body glazed with sweat, a sweat that gushed, it seemed to him, from his forehead, his cheeks, his temples, his scalp, his whole skull. He stared through the window, inert, at the building across the way, a one-story house that he couldn't take his eyes off.

Max comes calling one night. He is so alarmed by his friend's state of exhaustion that, without telling Franz, he writes a letter to Milena with strict instructions to be gentle with their friend: "His illness is much worse, did you not know?"

After nightfall, when the summer air has cooled and when he has stopped coughing, Franz sits down at his desk. His migraines notwithstanding, he composes a detailed account of his various errands, interjecting little jokes, punchy remarks about this person and that, in the hopes of eliciting some signs of gratitude, a smile, a compliment, from Professor Milena.

Who raps him on the head with her ruler.

"How can the soul relieve its oppression except with a little meanness?" he writes her. Realizing her ingratitude, she apologizes by telegram. Too late. He is dazed by her unreason. He can no longer draw the venom from her reproaches, which arrive in bursts. He can no longer bring himself to read Milena's letters. He prays for the young woman to disappear out the window, as he no longer has the strength to live with a hurricane in his bedroom.

Resentment, remorse, exhaustion, the end of an illusion—that, most likely, is what was brewing in Gmünd.

One among a thousand possible scenes: Kafka fears this meeting so much that he hasn't slept for several days. When he gets off the train, his legs wobble with anxiety. Milena walks toward him, she is wearing his favorite dress, the good-bye dress. At the sight of this man with graying hair and a slow walk, who looks at her with staring eyes (he wants to say: "Milena, by walking toward me you are plunging into the abyss"), this young woman, twenty-four years old, draws back in spite of herself. The man in Gmünd is not the man in Vienna, the tender, gay, alert lover whom she had adored. The man extending his arms to her is gravely ill. The enormous, the irresistible disappointment she feels is immediately reflected in the face of the stranger confronting her.

Six hours together, first stretched out on a patch of grass, then, when it starts to rain, lying like statues on a bed with suspect sheets in a shabby hotel by the station, a hotel for traveling salesmen.

Franz, his eyes shut, holds tightly to Milena's hand as though afraid of drowning. She does not bare her shoulder, he does not touch his lips to her naked breast. She caresses his face as though caressing a child with fever. Between the silences, he returns to the same subject.

"If you were unable, or unwilling, to leave your husband although your marriage was going badly, it isn't because Ernst is sick or because you're dependent on him. It's to avoid living with me. I am your scourge, and instead of separating you from your husband, I have brought you closer together, a truth that obsesses me. The rest is just lies. Let's stop talking about the future, we'll never live together, never even live in the same city. Let's think only about the present."

"Stop torturing me!" she says.

"I've told you many times, Milena, I do nothing but suffer torture and inflict it."

"What is the reason for this?"

"To wrest truth from myself, extort confession."

Before leaving the room, the young woman may have lingered in the bathroom. Wracked by remorse, by guilt, she remembers Max's letter asking her to treat Franz gently. She hasn't heeded this warning, she has constantly heaped reproaches on him, she tells herself he is going to die soon, he doesn't have the capacity to live. Franz is the only man in the world who never accepts a compromise. No one has the enormous strength he has, his undeviating need for truth. His purity.

On their return to the station, Franz decides to send a postcard to Ottla, his sister, friend, and confidante. Why the card, when it will arrive after him? To leave some proof of his meeting with Milena? He is so tired that he declares the task beyond him. Making his proof even stronger, he asks Milena to write out a line or two of dictation. Below, she writes: "He was unable to finish. Yours, cordially." Ottla kept this card, on which Milena's handwriting appears, but not her signature—a married woman's caution.

After Gmünd, she goes to Saint-Gilgen for a rest. During the two weeks of her stay and through the long month of November, Franz and Milena ask themselves the same question: Why is our relationship coming to an end?

Kafka attributes the problem to himself.

"But the real reason," he tells her, "is the inability to get beyond these letters. A thousand letters from you, a thousand wishes from me, won't change a thing."

Once again he speaks to her of his fear, a fear that extends to everything: fear of what's big, fear of what's small, fear of night, fear of not-night, a convulsive fear of uttering a single word, fear of venturing into a world bristling with traps, fear of the future, fear of everything that lives without modesty, fear of being abandoned, an awful fear of suffering. And above all, fear of never being equal to what is expected of him, an insurmountable fear of disappointing the women he loves, a nagging worry of impotence. When they made love on the grass in Vienna, he had felt his throat constrict several times. When fear overcame him, Milena would look him in the eyes, together they would wait a moment, he would recover his breath, and everything would once more become simple and clear.

To Milena, and only to Milena, he gives an account of his first sexual experience, which, he claims, is at the root of his sexual fears. He is twenty years old and a law student. On a hot summer day, as he is beating his brains out to learn a chapter on Roman law by heart, he looks out the window and sees the salesgirl from the candy store across the street. She is getting a breath of air on the sidewalk. The girl looks at him, he looks at her. They smile at each other. Using hand signals they agree to meet. At eight o'clock when he arrives she is talking to a man with whom she walks off, signaling Franz to follow. The two sit in a cafe, where they order a beer. Franz takes a nearby table and does the same. The couple then sets off toward the girl's house with Franz following.

For him it is irritating, exciting, horrible. The man leaves. Shortly after, Franz and the salesgirl go to a hotel. They emerge only at dawn. He sees her again two days later. His body, which has been in agonies for months, is contented, happy. Franz leaves on vacation not long afterward. On his return, he cannot bear to see the girl, pleasant though she is, he cannot say a word to her or offer her an excuse, nothing.

Why? At the hotel, the girl, all unconsciously, had made a nasty gesture—a gesture, he tells Milena, there is no call to specify. And she had said something dirty to him, also not worth mentioning. Yet both excited him frantically.

Afterward, his body—he talks about it as though it were an object in his keeping—was overtaken at irregular intervals by a keen desire, the desire for this dirty, repulsive something. The memory of these two bits of filth, the little gesture and the little phrase, was never erased, and for a long time he thought that this sordidness and horror were an integral part of the whole. The memory of it stayed with him forever after, a bad smell, a whiff of sulfur, a bit of hell lingering in the heart of pleasure.

"It is a little thing that determined my sexual life, just as in the great battles of history," he jokes, "where the fate of little things has been decided by little things."

Only in his journals does he confess his taste for brothels: "I walked by the brothel as though it were the house of a beloved," he writes. On his daily walks through Prague, he chooses streets with prostitutes. It excites him to walk past them.

Sometimes he accosts one. In June there were six in all. He knows nothing more agreeable or more innocent than the fulfillment of this desire, he feels no remorse about it. He is drawn to large and slightly older girls, wearing unfashionable clothes whose flounces and furbelows give them something of an air of luxury. Or girls with hefty behinds. There is one that nobody apart from himself would find at all attractive. She stands on the street corner in a tight-fitting yellow coat. When he encounters her, he turns around several times to look back at her. Yesterday he saw a girl who was truly ugly. He was quite drawn to her all the same.

With Max Brod in Paris he visited brothels. He describes their organization, the electric bell at the front door. He finds the drawing rooms too crowded with girls, who hem you in too closely and make it hard to choose.

"I can't understand how I found myself back on the street, can't understand how it all happened so quickly."

Did pleasure come too quickly?

Since coming to know Milena, he is no longer drawn absurdly into a world of squalor. His longing for sordidness has gone. He is no longer afraid.

Actually, in Gmünd, his fear returned at the very thought that Milena might never be his. He lost her.

On November 20, 1920, he ends their exchange of love letters. Milena accedes. Her hope, she says, is simply to separate from him completely.

In mid-December he flees. On his doctor's advice, he checks in to a sanatorium in Matliary, a resort in the

Tatra Mountains at three thousand feet. Its clientele includes the ailing, but also tourists, who come to hunt. Extending his leave of absence again and again, Franz stays there for ten months, until August 26, 1921.

To Max Brod, to Ottla, to his friends, he sends lively descriptions—written with such gaiety!—of the rooms he lives in before finally finding one that suits him. He offers portraits of the other guests, some thirty in number, and relates their conversation. He is an adept and genuine listener, and his tablemates speak freely before him. Mealtime discussions are often fueled by anti-Semitism. The legendary pusillanimity of the Jews is a frequent target, the cowardly subterfuges they used to avoid conscription during the war. "As to Jews who are also Communists," he writes Max, "they are drowned in the soup and carved up with the roast. Everyone laughs appreciatively, then apologizes to me once more."

He describes his diet in detail (liters of milk and cream but no meat, which inflames his hemorrhoids). He complains (again, as always) of the noise coming from the kitchen, the restaurant, the other rooms, the next-door balcony "where a young man (what a race!) hums Hebraic melodies, his hand thrust into his fly."

To escape this cacophony that is driving him mad—his hearing, made keen by anxiety, picks up everything—he takes refuge, as he had at Zürau earlier, with Ottla, in a lovely prairie surrounded by woods, an island between two streams. There, steeped in silence like a fish in an aquarium, he wonders if the noises made by his neighbors irritate him because they point to the emptiness of his own existence and the solitude he revels in.

To Max alone, he mentions his state of health, the boils on his buttocks that are so deeply embedded they won't heal, his flirtations, two walks with a young lady in the forest, nothing happened, he says, just a few long looks; the violent snowstorm that has been raging for two weeks and has pinned him deep in his bed. His fever is rising, he can no longer read, nor write, nor sleep, nor stay awake, he is too worn out, he coughs constantly. As he is recovering from this bout of influenza, he is pole-axed by intestinal fever.

The letters from Matliary resemble the stylistic exercises from Zürau, in which he described his epic struggle against the mouse people. One of them tells of visiting a neighboring patient, a Czech with tuberculosis of the larynx. The man invites him into his room one day and explains in a cavernous voice how, using mirrors, he captures the rays of the sun to irradiate the ulcers in the back of his throat, at the risk of burning himself severely. He then opens his mouth wide to display his sores to his visitor. Kafka feels himself sinking into a faint, as though a wave were breaking over him. Seeing nothing, hearing nothing, using the walls of the room to guide himself, he flees onto the balcony, where he recovers somewhat in the cold air. He then exits the patient's room without really taking his leave. Just a few words, "What a lovely evening!" to explain his outing onto the balcony, and "I feel quite tired" to justify his exit.

What he saw in that bed, he says, is "far more terrible than an execution, worse even than torture. All the misery of that life—the fever, the suffocation, the mirrors, the drug taking—has no other goal than to prolong the torture, which the patient freely inflicts on himself. And to this slow-burning pyre come parents, doctors, and visitors who cool and refresh the torture victim, console him, encourage him to endure further suffering. Then once back in their rooms, terrified, they wash their hands—as I have just done."

There are others in Matliary besides patients at death's door. Franz encounters young ladies, healthy young men, pretty serving girls, and numerous tourists. In February he develops a genuine friendship with one of the other guests, Robert Klopstock, a young man of twenty-one who has interrupted his medical studies to care for his lungs, which are lightly affected by tuberculosis. A native of Budapest, he is ambitious, intelligent, and literary, a tall man, wide of girth, blond, with pink cheeks. He is almost too corpulent (especially compared to Franz, who is having trouble regaining the pounds he lost earlier). Robert comes to Franz's room every night to wrap him with the utmost care in cold-water compresses. They talk for hours. Franz grows more and more interested in the young man. He asks Ottla to send him books, drawn, as he specifies, from his own library.

He writes to Max: "Can you help him with his career? He is Jewish but no, he is not a Zionist. Dostoyevsky and Jesus are his masters."

Since the letter of November 20, Milena has heard nothing further from him. Breaking her promise to Max, she writes Franz. He answers with just a few lines: "Don't write to me and avoid any chance that we might meet. Do this, I beg you, without saying another word. Only this will let me go on living a little, the rest can only destroy me."

Milena obeys but, toward mid-April, on a difficult night, she writes him again. She implores him to give her news of himself one last time. He learns from Max that, seriously ill, she has reconciled herself with her father and gone to live with him. He immediately writes Max: "Let me know when she will be in Prague and for how long, I do not want to run into her."

Despite his resolve, he sees Milena again in late August. And in early October, he entrusts her with his thirteen large notebooks (she is the only other person to have read his *Diaries*, perhaps the only other person to have held them in her hands, during his lifetime). In late November, she comes to visit him four times at home. At this point, he hardly ever rises from bed. The visits are affectionate and dignified, but a bit weary, a bit stilted, as sickbed visits are.

In the lobby she encounters his parents. They greet her icily, Hermann Kafka in particular, who mutters under his breath as she goes by.

When Franz looks at the young woman sitting across from him, he remembers their first meeting at the Café Arco.

He thinks: I am a live memory, that is one cause of my insomnia, always Milena, or perhaps not Milena, but a light in the shadows.

Did the shadows hold the memory of a humiliation that he never explicitly admitted?

Does it not seem strange that in all the letters Kafka writes to Milena (some 150) there is no echo of any admiration on her part for his work? Whereas he heaps praise on the most trivial of her newspaper articles.

It was after reading *The Stoker*, *The Metamorphosis*, and *A Country Doctor* that Milena decided to translate them. And it was these texts that, like Ariadne's thread, led her to Kafka and bound her to him.

During the months she worked on them, she sought the most faithful Czech equivalent for each of the words he had written, attentive to the rhythms of the sentences and the author's hidden intentions. No one, consequently, had read the texts more attentively than she.

She submits each of her translations to him. He immediately congratulates her, praises her, calls her "Professor Milena." He dreams of being her student, assures her that she has transformed his "bad, his extraordinarily bad stories" and made them readable. He hardly dares to bring up a few egregious mistranslations.

At the beginning of their correspondence in May, he tells "Dear Frau Milena" the story of Fyodor Dostoyevsky's first success. The Russian writer has just finished his first novel, *Poor Folk*. His roommate, Grigorowitsch, also a writer, reads it at once and is entranced by it. He steals the manuscript and runs off to show it to

the most celebrated critic in Russia. At four in the morning Dostoyevsky's doorbell rings. It is his friend with the
great critic, Nekrasov, who, meeting Dostoyevsky for the
first time, embraces him, kisses him on the cheek, and
calls him "Russia's hope." They spend two hours together,
talking mostly about the novel.

Kafka adds that Dostoyevsky, who would later remember this as one of the great nights of his life, leans out the
window and watches the two men as they walk away at
dawn. Choked with emotion, he starts to cry, repeating
over and over: "What splendid men! How good they are,
how noble, to have come during the night without waiting. Oh, how wonderful that is, how noble!"

That is not all.

On August 1, Franz dreams of Milena, a sad dream,
which he tells her about in great detail. They are walking together on a street in Prague. Milena, her face heavily powdered, and the powder clumsily applied, is acting
coldly toward him. The cause of her coolness he does
not know. They meet a man at the cafe who looks like
Dostoyevsky and who responds openly, cordially, amply,
whenever Franz asks him a question. And who ignores
him each time he stops questioning him.

These two stories have no effect. Milena refuses to play
the part of Nekrasov. Tired of waiting for a compliment,

or even a word of encouragement, he settles for a reproof: "Scold me thoroughly," he writes, "for you know how to do everything, but scold me better than the rest."

Whereas he upbraided Felice for offering no reaction to his first collection, Franz doesn't dare question Milena directly. They discuss literature. Robert Louis Stevenson, about whom Kafka knows nothing, is Milena's favorite author, along with Chekhov. Franz also admires Chekhov, at times passionately. On the other hand, he disparages a novel that Milena has several times urged him to read and praised to the skies: *Marie Donadieu*.[16]

He continues nonetheless to extend opportunities to her. He tells her with what haste, what emotion, he has read each of her articles, he can't stand to miss a single one. He offers comments on them, keeps them like precious relics. He buys a dozen copies of each, as he does with her translations of his stories.

He sends her his "Letter to His Father." In early October 1921 he gives her the bulky blue notebooks of his *Diaries*, of which even Max has read only rare passages.

Franz is waiting, one would swear, for Milena to swoon and send flowers. Yet once again she says nothing. The proof? On January 20, 1922, four months later, he asks

---

16 By the French social realist Charles-Louis Philippe (1874–1909).

her this question: "Did you find something decisive against me in the *Diaries*?"

He perhaps wonders if Milena even took the trouble to open his notebooks. Might she have stuffed them into some corner of her vast armoire and forgotten them?

Does he decide to fish for a criticism, if only to make her read his heart laid bare?

On January 18, 1923, although he is gravely ill, he writes her an interminable letter of congratulations, verging on flattery. He has just read Milena's "The Devil at the Hearth." He cannot find the words to express his admiration: "A marvelous and moving article, in which the dazzling character of your thoughts is striking, touching."

In opposition to Max, Oskar, Felix, and Ernst, who howled with appreciative laughter at Franz's reading of "The Metamorphosis" and the first chapters of *The Trial*, women, at least those who fall in love with him, find that his works depict a world where man is only a pitiful shadow under the sun, a world of absurdity where every undertaking is destined to failure, where the innocent accept their guilt, where even the emperor's messenger cannot deliver his message because "if he were ever to reach the bottom of the stairs, he would be no farther along, as he would still have to cross the courtyards. And after the courtyards, the second palace surrounding them, and then more stairs and courtyards, and after them a further palace. And so on for centuries and centuries." Chilled to the bone, Franz's women no longer know the man they love, can no longer separate fiction from fact.

And yet . . . immediately following Kafka's death, Milena published an obituary that one cannot read, and reread, without being deeply moved. An admirable analysis of the man and his work, one of the most sensitive ever written.[17]

O n May 8, 1922, he sees Milena for the last time. Their encounter stays with him like a sore that won't heal.

"Don't be unhappy," he tells himself in the *Diaries*. "Don't put any pressure on yourself, but don't be unhappy that you are putting no pressure on yourself, stop sniffing voluptuously at the opportunity for pressure."

Despite his sermons, he is clearly in distress.

The question that haunts him is whether, since he was happy with Felice in Marienbad, he might not now find happiness with Milena in Prague. After their painful breakup in Gmünd.

---

17 An extract can be found on pages 257–58.

He doubts it. Between himself and Milena is not a wall but a grave. Yet sexual desire inflames him, tortures him day and night. "To satisfy it," he writes, "I would have to overcome my fear, my sense of modesty, and also my sadness."

Rejected by Milena, banished, expelled from the world and the company of the living, incapable—as he believes—of forming bonds with anyone, he buries himself. He disappears into silence, the darkness of his burrow, the only place where he feels safe. In nine months, with the tracery of his pen, he builds *The Castle*,[18] his third and final novel, the most personal, the most allegorical, the novel that makes one wonder: Is it the memory of a disillusion that hovers on the heights?

---

18 *The Castle*, unfinished at Kafka's death, was published by Kurt Wolff in Munich in 1926. Of the print run of 1,500 copies, few were sold.

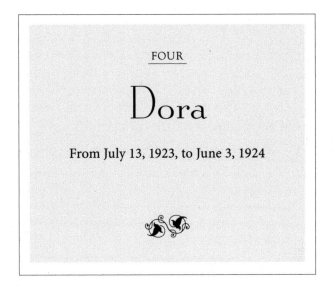

FOUR

Dora

From July 13, 1923, to June 3, 1924

"If I reach my fortieth year, then I'll probably marry an old maid with protruding upper teeth, left a little exposed by the upper lip."

—DIARY ENTRY

The Young Girl and Death

When he asks himself about his own identity, Franz Kafka recognizes that he is a Jew among non-Jews, a nonbeliever among believers, a German among Czechs. True, he writes in German, but never without the feeling that he is appropriating something that doesn't belong to him. His hind legs, he says, are still stuck to the language of his forefathers.

In May 1917, which is the year he contracts tuberculosis, the year of his final break with Felice, Kafka becomes more involved with Judaism. Three years earlier he had said that he had nothing in common with the

Jews, he barely had anything in common with himself. But in 1917 he is closely following the cultural and political trends affecting Prague's Jewish intellectuals. He subscribes to the Zionist periodical *Selbstwehr* (Self-defense), which is edited by his friend, the philosopher Felix Weltsch.[19] As each issue appears, he devours it from start to finish. He has avidly read all three volumes of Heinrich Graetz's *Popular History of the Jews*.

He starts to learn Hebrew, at first on his own, using the forty-five lessons in the manual by Moses Rath. Then he turns to a series of professors. The first is Georg Mordecai Langer, who has ostentatiously cast off his Western education and now wears the dress and leads the life of a Hasid. The second is Rabbi Friedrich Thieberger, a Zionist philologist with a passion for photography. The third is a young woman originally from Jerusalem, Puah Ben Tovim.

The three teach him the secular language forged by the Lithuanian visionary Eliezer Ben-Yehuda. An immigrant to Palestine, Ben-Yehuda had been battling since

---

19 After working as librarian at Prague University, Weltsch emigrated to Palestine, where he became a librarian at Jerusalem University. He died in that city in 1964.

the Balfour Declaration in November 1917 to have Hebrew declared the national language. By contrast, Theodor Herzl thought the language spoken in the Promised Land ought to be German.

Of the three teachers, Franz prefers Puah, because he feels more at ease with a young woman, because Hebrew is her mother tongue, and because she is the first bird of passage to arrive from Palestine. She comes to his house three times a week to conduct classes in his bedroom. Whenever Franz coughs, Frau Kafka comes running anxiously to the door. The sight of her son, his eyes choked with tears, stops her in her tracks. She withdraws, her head drooping. Puah doesn't know whether to continue the lesson, as her pupil insists, or to interrupt it, as his mother would like.

He works so obstinately at his studies that he is soon attempting to read a novel by Brenner, *Sterility and Failure*, a difficult book and one not particularly to his liking. He can only read a page of it a day. But he takes wholehearted pleasure in Puah's description of her life in Palestine and her job teaching mathematics in Prague, where she has come to spend the year. The young woman has the gift of leaving a little of her gaiety in her wake, and a little of her serene confidence.

Over the months, he fills five notebooks with grammar exercises and columns of vocabulary, with the German word on the left and the Hebrew on the right.[20] On ten scattered sheets are the starts of stories, some letters in Hebrew, some doodles and sketches. Rescuing a threatened identity and the collective memory of a people now seems important to him.[21]

Every so often, in the manner of a recurring dream, he makes plans to emigrate to Palestine. His health would improve in the dry and sunny climate of the Mediterranean, and life would be relatively inexpensive. His favorite fruits, cherries, bananas, and strawberries, would be on the table every day. In Prague their cost is exorbitant. And the cost of living is too often ignored.

In October 1922, encouraged by Else Bergmann, the wife of another Hebrew student, he seriously considers taking the plunge. Is it not reasonable to leave Prague, rife as it is with anti-Semitism? Is it not natural to leave a place where one is the object of such hatred? To stay

---

20 Puah Ben Tovim donated the Hebrew notebook Kafka left her to the National Library of Israel.

21 Neither his notebooks nor his letters in Hebrew have been published. Following his custom, Franz started his notebooks at both ends, with the two texts meeting in the middle (he often did the same in writing his *Diaries*).

despite everything, he says, is to emulate the heroism of the cockroach, which nothing can drive from the bathroom.

The Czech newspaper *Venkov* serves its readers a daily diet of stories about the Jewish people over the centuries. All of them illustrate the great lack of fortitude of the Jews, their cowardice, their greed, their treacherousness. One night in mid-November, Franz watches from his window as mounted police and gendarmes with fixed bayonets disperse a crowd that has been attacking Jewish shops shouting, "Mangy race of Jews!" He is ashamed at having to live under police protection.

When he passes in front of the Jewish town hall and sees the hundreds of Russian and Polish immigrants queuing for visas to America, he wishes he were among those carefree children soon to cross the Atlantic. He knows that, like Moses, he will never enter the Land of Canaan. It is a fantasy, such as a person might have who knows that he will never leave his bed. But does one ever really know? Out of nothing, something whole can come.

Besides, one has to find a reason to hope.

In the meantime, Franz labors at the promised language, the writing of his ancestors.

His father did not hand down to him any religious instruction. Franz did celebrate his bar mitzvah at the Gypsy Synagogue on June 13, 1896.[22] The day of Milena's birth.

In October 1911, at the Café Arco, the most ordinary cafe in Prague, he met Yitzhak Löwy, an actor trying to revive the Yiddish language through his plays and lectures. Kafka became his most ardent admirer and would gladly have kneeled down in the dust to applaud him. He helped Löwy in every way he could, applying on his behalf for subsidies, selling tickets to his performances, and giving two lectures, one of them on Yiddish, the youngest European language, and the other on the Jewish theater.

In the second lecture, he introduces a personal reminiscence. When he was fourteen, he says, on a day when his parents thought him at synagogue, bent over the pages of the Talmud, he went to the theater for the first time to see Meyerbeer's *Les Huguenots*. He was electrified. Yiddish theater mixes drama, tragedy, song, comedy, dance, everything together, it is life itself, he exclaims![23] He can no longer do without it. Even if it means telling lies and committing sins.

---

22 The photograph of Franz taken on that day, an original silver negative (45 by 36 mm), was sold at auction in Paris on November 18, 2010, for 15,000 euros.

23 American musical comedy apparently grew out of the Yiddish theater.

His two speeches cost him many nights of insomnia. He doesn't have the actor's superb effrontery, which allows him to exhibit himself and stand firm under the gaze of an audience. But no one else is willing to stand up and speak. Löwy, hot-tempered and resentful, has few friends and barely earns a living. His performances are never well attended.

When Hermann Kafka finds the actor visiting Franz in his house, he grows furious. His lips tighten into a line, his head shakes ironically, he reproaches his son for befriending a stranger who has nothing to offer, a vermin who would lead you back to Yiddish, the language of the poor and the backward. Our language, he says, is German, and our culture is German culture. He even forbids his son to invite this flea-ridden specimen to share a meal with them, his presence is an affront, intolerable.

"I don't care if that Pole does hear me from your room. All your friends are good-for-nothings."

Even Max Brod, the most brilliant and prominent intellectual in Prague, fails to find favor in Hermann's eyes. Just yesterday, he had called his son's inseparable friend a *meschuggenner ritoch,* a Yiddish expression meaning "crazy hothead." Hermann Kafka is oblivious to his own contradictions. When he is angry, he turns to his mother tongue, the only one that was spoken in his wretched shtetl. Now that he is a prominent resident of Prague, the owner of a flourishing business, he is an Austrian citizen and nothing else.

All the more reason for Franz to learn Hebrew.

In early July 1923, he sets off for Müritz, a beach resort on the Baltic, for a rest. He has asked his eldest sister Elli to accompany him. He no longer feels capable of traveling or living alone, in Müritz or anywhere else.

They stay at the Haus Glickauf Hotel, where his room is right next to the room that Elli shares with her two children, Felix and Gerti. He is happy to be close to the sea. He hasn't seen it for ten years. He finds it more beautiful, more varied, more alive, fresher. He writes his friends to tell them.

From his balcony, where sparrows have built their nest under the balustrade, he looks out through a belt of pines and birch trees to where children play along the shore. The children are blond, with blue eyes, they are healthy and run all over the place merrily. They live in a two-story house, Haus Huten. It is a vacation camp organized by the Jewish People's Home in Berlin, the same organization where Felice, his first fiancée, agreed to volunteer a few years earlier. The memory of Felice no longer torments him, it is so distant. She married a few months after their final separation and now has two sons. Ottla keeps him informed.

For half the day and night, the forest, the sea, and the air around Haus Huten are filled with children's singing. Elli meets the young women who work as camp counselors, all of whom are volunteers, and Felix and Gerti soon join the camp activities.

In the early afternoon, Franz goes down to the beach and plays with the children. These orphans from Russia and Poland, he writes, so vigorous, so passionate, and whom he speaks to in Hebrew, give him a sense of being on the verge of happiness.

One of the camp counselors, named Tile Rössler, is a lively, engaging adolescent, so thin, so frail, it is hard to believe she is even sixteen. She is also the only one to know who Dr. Kafka is. She worked part time at the Jurovics bookstore in Berlin, and she had put one of his books, *The Stoker*, on display in the shop window. She says that the Berlin critics are full of praise for the book, and that Dr. Kafka occupies an important position in Prague.

One day, late in the afternoon when he is playing with the children from the People's Home, Tile introduces herself. He listens to her. She launches on a long narrative, happily answering his questions about the children, the organization of the camp, herself and her life in Berlin, the bookstore. And this man whom everyone admires for his elegance—he even dresses with care to go to the beach—this man addresses her using the informal *Du.*

Ever since, she has been on the lookout for him. As soon as she sees him sit down on the sand or walk, his blanket folded over his arm, toward his deck chair at the end of the jetty, she races to sit at his feet. And they resume their conversation. One day she says, "You see, I speak every language, only I speak it in Yiddish," and she is proud to have made him laugh.

She has the idea of offering him a present. But what? She decides to make a clay pot for him in the children's pottery workshop. When it comes out of the kiln, she paints it. Pleased with the result, she goes to the Haus Glickauf to give it to Dr. Kafka. She has sent word of her visit beforehand.

She waits in the lobby for him to come down from his room. A pianist with a blond mane is playing a Grieg sonata. The concierge is reading the newspaper. An elderly couple at a table near the bar sip glasses of white wine.

Dr. Kafka would later tell her that he had a perfectly clear memory of her on that day: "Leaning a little forward, a little abstracted, you were listening to the sonata by Grieg, bowing humbly to the music."

He walks toward her saying, "I, too, have a present for you."

Tile, flushed with emotion, has trouble stripping the tissue paper from the object he has handed her. As she tears at the wrapping, he says, "We should always take hold of delicate objects delicately."

A ruby-colored glass cup filled with chocolates trembles in Tile's hands.

She throws herself into his arms and rests her head on his chest.

"How did you know?"

The adolescent has been eyeing this cup in the pastry shop window, where it sparkled and glowed next to the plum tarts. Dr. Kafka had seen the girl and her friend Sabine with their noses pressed to the glass. As he walked past, he heard Tile say, "I'll never be able to buy myself such a lovely thing."

"You'll smash this cup on your wedding day," he says. "And I'll always keep your vase. I won't give it to anyone."

Since receiving this extravagant present, Tile has been walking on air, singing the praises of her older friend.

On Friday, July 12, with the enthusiastic agreement of the other members of the home, Tile invites Dr.

Kafka to join them for Sabbath dinner, to be followed by a show.

When he arrives at the oddly shaped house at the end of the afternoon, he enters the wrong door and finds himself in the kitchen, which is flooded with light from the setting sun. Bees circle in the heavy golden air and knock against the windowpanes. Franz's attention is drawn to the bowed neck of a young woman scaling fish. Seeing her pull the entrails from a salmon, he says, "Such lovely hands to do such bloody work!"[24]

The counselor turns, recognizes him. Her face grows red. She has seen him several times on the beach with his family all around him. She curtsies and introduces herself: "Dora Diamant." She adds, "I know who you are. Tile talks of no one but you, and the home has been buzzing since this morning."

She asks after his wife and children. He laughs: "My wife? My children?"

Her mistaken assumption and the amusement it provides perhaps cement the attraction they already feel for each other.

------

24 In *The Castle*, when K. meets Frieda, who has come to feed the animals, he says to her, "With such delicate hands?" and he asks himself "if it is just flattery or if he has been smitten by hands that are, after all, perfectly ordinary."

After dinner, Dora recites the forty-third chapter of Isaiah: "Fear not: for I have redeemed thee." She comments on the passage. Dr. Kafka, amazed by her knowledge of Hebrew and Judaism, can't take his eyes off her.

The next day, and the days after that, he visits the home again.

Tile soon realizes that he has eyes only for the Polish girl. At mealtimes, he takes the seat next to her. On the beach, Tile sees them engaged in endless conversations. Since she introduced him to the home, he has shifted his attention to this plump young woman who speaks and reads Hebrew so well. All day the flat, skinny adolescent follows them at a distance. She sees them walk along the flowering dunes or out on the jetty into the lapping sound of the waves.

She surprises them sitting side by side, sheltering from the wind, their heads drawn together as they recite from a Hebrew text, their eyes meeting above the book.

Do they take themselves for a pair of mythical lovers, for Francesca and Paolo da Rimini?

Toward the end of July, Tile returns to Berlin, from where she writes two letters to her friend. Franz sends her a long reply on August 3.[25] It is the affectionate, light-hearted letter of an older brother to his younger sister. So that there should be no misunderstanding, he talks to her about Dora, a "marvelous creature."

The life story of this "marvelous creature" fascinates him, as the life story of the actor Löwy had earlier. Born in Poland, Dora fled her father's house at the age of eighteen. She ran away from Bedzin and its imposing synagogue, which looms over the town and the castle.[26]

Freed from Hasidic law, which imposes so many duties and restrictions on women and affords them so few rights, Dora lives for a year in Breslau. There she starts to read literature and study German, all the while working in a kindergarten. From there she emigrates to Berlin, the City of Light, with its population of 170, 000 Jews, many of whom play important roles in the social and cultural life of the city. The two largest newspaper groups, Ullstein and Mosse, are owned by Jews.

---

25 When Tile Rössler emigrated to Palestine, where she became a choreographer, she took this letter with her, as well as the brief note that accompanied the box of candies and the ruby cup that Kafka had given her.

26 When the Germans overran Bedzin in September 1939, they set fire to the synagogue, where hundreds of families had taken shelter. The building was reduced to ashes, and there were no survivors. A few blackened stones from the synagogue serve as a memorial to this massacre.

Dora works at several jobs and volunteers at the People's Home. Brave and determined (the two qualities Kafka admires most), she is wonderfully young (a little more than twenty), intelligent, gentle, devout, pious, and in excellent health. And she takes care of children. Blessings on this meeting!

In the course of their talks, she tries to instill Franz with her strength: "Do what you have always wanted to do, leave Prague and move to Berlin. In the spring, we'll emigrate to Palestine together. We'll open a restaurant in Tel Aviv, 'Spring Hill.'"

In early August he leaves Müritz and Dora. Arriving in Berlin, he attends a performance of Schiller's *The Robbers* on August 7, accompanied by Tile and two of her friends. The play makes little impression on him, other than to highlight his own exhaustion. The vacation in Müritz has done nothing to improve his health. He feels at the limit of his strength. He weighs 120 pounds, thinner than he has ever been.

Where better to go and gain weight than to his beloved sister Ottla? She has rented a vacation house in Schelesen, where she is living alone with her daughter, Vera, and her newborn, Helen.

He joins her there in mid-August and stays for more than a month. He realizes that, for the first time, he has forgotten her birthday. He has even forgotten the exact date, is it October 29 or October 30?

"As far as I am concerned," he says, "you don't grow any older. I don't believe in your being thirty-one years old." He adds, "Be glad you are a woman."

She is the only person he talks to about Dora and their plans. Ottla encourages him, as she always has, to free himself of his chains.

He is beset by doubts, assailed by forces antagonistic to him. He takes to his bed, feverish once more.

"Rain is leaking into the hovel," he tells his sister.

Scarcely fattened up, he returns to Prague, winds up his affairs in a day and a half, asks his employer for early retirement. He packs his bags, a horribly complicated business, he would never have seen it through without the help of "Fräulein," his beloved Marie Werner, the family's old and faithful governess. Against his father's advice (another quarrel!), under his mother's worried gaze, and despite the gloomy forecasts of his brother-in-law Pepa, he gathers the last remnants of his strength and flees to Berlin.

He has announced his arrival to Dora via telegram: "Will arrive Berlin Monday 24 September. Can you be at station?"

For how long is he going away? Four or five days? Certainly not much more.

He has climbed into the express train that sets off into the night. He savors his mad act of daring. The only comparison he can find is with Napoleon and his campaign into Russia. At the age of forty, he has managed to escape Prague, his family, the office, and the daily grind.

When he arrives in Berlin, to whom does he announce his incredible victory? To Milena, who has sent him a letter from Italy.

"Something wonderful has happened to me," he writes. "What wonderful things exist in the world! I live almost in the country, in a small villa with a garden. I have never lived in such a beautiful apartment, I am afraid of losing it, it is much too beautiful for me."

He goes on to say that while at the beach on the Baltic he met a worker from the Jewish Home and that he has followed her to Berlin: "I am well and tenderly looked after, to the limit of possibility here on earth."

Is it likely that Milena received this news with a quiet heart, this picture of Franz happy in another's arms?

The villa with a garden that he writes Milena about was found by Dora in the residential district of Steglitz, at number 8 on elegant Miquelstrasse.

When he ventures out on a warm evening to stroll along the avenues lined with splendid residences, the smells from the lush, old gardens wash over him with a sweetness and intensity he has experienced nowhere else, neither in Schelesen nor Merano nor Marienbad. He hardly strays beyond the immediate vicinity of the villa. The botanical gardens are a fifteen-minute walk away, the Grünewald forest only a little farther.

A profound peace rules over this patrician suburb, the children he meets look healthy, beggars are scarce and not threatening at all.

But there are rumblings from the center of Berlin. The news is horrible, horrible. Constant uprisings and strikes, factories closing every day, businesses going bankrupt, thousands of the unemployed demonstrating. Inflation spirals upward so dizzyingly that prices no longer rise from day to day but from hour to hour. A newspaper that cost 100,000 marks in August costs 150 million marks in September, and a loaf of bread costs four million marks. Hunger riots erupt across the country. One night, four bodies are carted off the streets of Berlin. Desperate mobs loot shops and corporate businesses. The whole nation sinks into poverty. The nationalist party blames the Treaty of Versailles and the huge debt that Germany has been saddled with, in order to crush it forever.

Franz's retirement pension of a thousand marks is no longer enough, despite a very advantageous exchange rate. His monthly payments arrive weeks behind schedule. He is forced, with bowed head, to ask his parents and sisters, Ottla in particular, to lend him small sums. And to send him supplies of sugar, butter (he eats a great deal of it to gain weight), honey, kefir, marmalade, tea, and chocolate from warm and well-stocked Bohemia.

He can't manage to make ends meet, and because of his illness he has greater needs than others. When they run out of alcohol fuel, Dora warms their dinner over candle stubs.

Max peppers him with questions, but he refuses to talk about Dora. None of his friends can know that they are living together, a young woman's reputation is at stake. His letters only glancingly allude to Fräulein Diamant.

———

That fall starts off warm and bright. Franz pushes his walks as far as the botanical garden. He inhales the smell of the linden trees in flower, tours the tropical greenhouses, charts the changing colors of the foliage, and, along the silent walkways, hears the crinkling under his feet of the first dead leaves.

One day as he enters through the gates of the park, he sees a young girl sobbing. He walks up to her. She is one of those little blond flowers with white skin and red cheeks that grow so abundantly in these parts. He asks her, "Why are you crying?"

"I've lost my doll."

"You haven't lost it," he says.

"Did you find it?"

"No, no, I didn't find it. Your doll went off on a trip."

"How do you know that?"

"She wrote me a letter."

"Show me."

"I left it at home. But if you like, I'll bring it tomorrow, at three o'clock. Right here in front of this bench."

"What's your name?"

"Franz. And yours?"

"Malou."

Once back at his house, he asks himself what Ottla would say to her eldest daughter if by a stroke of bad luck the girl lost her doll, Lolotte, which she clutches to her heart even when she is sound asleep.

The following day at the appointed time, Malou and Franz meet in front of the bench. He raises his hat in greeting and hands her an envelope, on which he has written her name and stuck a canceled stamp.

Malou shrugs: "I don't know how to read."

He reads it for her. The doll ends her letter with the words "Many hugs and kisses, I'll write you every day."

Malou thinks for a moment before asking, "Does that mean you'll bring me another letter tomorrow?"

The next day and every day after, Franz brings her a new letter. As he starts to read, Malou's heart races. Her doll is going to the theater, to the cinema, to the circus, to the opera, to Vienna, to Paris, she is riding horseback, dancing, singing in an orchestra, it makes your head whirl.

Now the park trees raise their black branches into the low, dark sky. A cold wind swirls along the walkways and lifts great sprays of coppery leaves into the air like clouds of birds. A wool hat jammed onto her head, her hands deep in her coat pockets, Malou watches them distractedly. Franz, despite his woolens, his overcoat, and his big scarf, trembles with the cold. He interrupts his reading often and walks rapidly away, a handkerchief pressed to his mouth.

"Stop coughing," says Malou. "Read me the rest."

She holds out a sticky candy she has fished from her pocket. He comes back and finishes the letter in a quieter, more quavering voice.

"You're reading too fast today. Start over. It's so wonderful."

The letters, like the days, grow shorter. Since her marriage, the doll has been so frightfully busy that she no longer finds the time to write. One day she announces that she is going to Tibet, which is so far away and perched so high that it is known as the Roof of the World. She will live in a village lost in the clouds, surrounded by snow and ice, to which no mailman ever climbs. "I'll no longer be able to write you, dear Malou, but I won't forget you," are her last words.

"Is the Roof of the World really very far?" asks Malou.

Before Franz can reply, she twirls her skip rope over her head and nimbly flies off.[27]

---

27 Kafka does not mention this meeting in any of his texts, nor the twenty or so letters that he wrote to console the young girl. He had often wanted to write a fairy tale, particularly in Riva. Did he feel, faced with this child, a moral obligation to distract her from her grief, knowing that he could? A fairy tale, after all, is not judged by the same criteria as a literary text. The story of the doll is told by Dora in the *Diary* that she wrote in London in 1951.

His landlady, a small, skinny woman who nonetheless wears a very tight corset, suddenly takes a dislike to him. On November 15, two months after they moved in, she evicts Franz and Dora, two insolvent foreigners. Their rent has gone up by a factor of ten because of inflation.

They find a pleasant apartment not too far away, at 13 Grünewaldstrasse, at the house of Herr Seifert.[28] But they abandon it for similar reasons on February 1, 1924. An icy wind is blowing on the day they move out to take up lodgings in Berlin-Zehlendorf, at 25 Heidestrasse. The landlady is Frau Busse, the widow of a writer. The rent is horrendously high, a third of a trillion!

Unable to buy anything, they live in extreme deprivation. They never go to the theater, it is far too expensive. They never buy the newspaper, not even the Sunday edition. All for the better, as the news is so catastrophic that they actually avoid walking past the Town Hall, where the daily paper is posted.

---

28 Of the three residences, it is the only one that survives. A plaque between the two windows on the ground floor commemorates the fact that Kafka lived there for three months.

Two or three times a week, Franz goes to the Institute for Jewish Studies. It is a haven of peace. An entire building, with nice well-heated lecture rooms, a large library, few students, a good teacher of the Talmud, Herr Guttmann, all for free.

So as to maintain contact with the suffering of the world, he ventures into the city occasionally. He returns with his face coated in dirt, as though from a battle. For the most part he rests, stretched out in the sun on the glass-enclosed veranda, while Dora takes classes in theater and dance at the Jewish Home, also for free.

At night, by candlelight, they play like children. Franz, using his agile hands to project shadows on the wall, creates characters and invents dramatic plays and comedies that make the two laugh until the tears come. Sometimes they amuse themselves by dipping their hands into a basin of water. It is their family bath. Or else Franz, with a tray full of glasses and plates balanced on his palm, glides around the room to train for becoming a waiter, a skill he will need when they open their restaurant in Tel Aviv.

Most often, to keep the young woman he loves under the spell of his charm, he reads to her from favorite authors. From Goethe, he reads particularly *Hermann and Dorothea*. From Kleist, *The Marquise of O*. As though bewitched, he reads this story to Dora, recites it, six times in a row.

"Why such a favorite?" she asks. "Is it the literary quality of the text?"

"Yes."

"The unusual story?"

"Yes, also."

Perhaps it is due even more to the author, with whom he shares so many affinities: the passion for writing, the search for truth, the desire to start a family, which ends in a broken engagement. Kleist also endured illness and repeated failures, and he had the elegance to burn all his private papers, drafts, and unfinished works.

By the lake at Riva, Franz had told Gerti about Pushkin's tragic end. Today, he narrates Kleist's to Dora. A death composed like a work of art.

Heinrich von Kleist loves Henriette, the wife of Louis Vogel, with whom she has had a child. And Henriette loves the young poet. Driven by a sublime need for the absolute, nothing in this world can satisfy them, Heinrich and Henriette enter a suicide pact. On the Wannsee in 1811, he is thirty-four, Kleist puts a bullet through Henriette, then turns the pistol on himself.

Franz reads Dora the two letters Henriette wrote on the eve of her death, one to her dear husband, the other to her closest friend: "Take care of my child." He recites his own favorite, Kleist's letter to his beloved sister Ulrike. Dora, her eyes full of tears, leans against the shoulder of the man she calls "my sweet love" and "my gentle Franz."

He writes to Max. To Ottla. He sends each new address to Felix Weltsch so as not to miss a single issue of *Selbstwehr*. His letters are few, stamps are expensive.

And he has started writing again.

A few friends visit him: Max has asked him to look after, distract, reason with, and console his mistress, Emmy Salveter, a former chambermaid, now an actress. Deeply in love, this ravishing young woman suffers enormously from Max's absence. She rebels against his sense of duty, which forbids him to marry her, and insists that he come to Berlin.

Franz receives her at home, while Dora is away, accompanies her on walks, visits her at her house. Too often, Emmy calls to say that she is coming over, then changes her mind at the last moment or else telephones to say that she will come at two instead of noon. She sets a date for her next visit, then catches a cold and doesn't come. She is deeply troubled, and the unrest in Berlin disturbs her so much that she transmits her anxieties to Franz, who must then spend the night fending them off.

One day, two handsome young people with charming manners knock at the apartment door. It is Tile Rössler with a young painter from Berlin. Tile stops dead on the threshold at the sight of Dora in a dressing gown.

Puah Ben Tovim, who came to spend an afternoon with them, was able to mark her pupil's progress in Hebrew.

On November 25, Ottla arrives. She has left Vera and Helen in the care of her husband for two days. She wants to see how her brother is doing with her own eyes and meet Dora, whom she knows only through letters and the telephone.

She is lugging a trunk with her, in which she has packed the linens and clothes that her brother asked her for, a long list! He left Prague thinking he would be gone only a few days and didn't bring his winter clothes. She unpacks three unstarched shirts, three pairs of ordinary socks and one warm pair, his black suit, his big overcoat, his old blue raglan coat, two pairs of long underwear, a lightweight sheet, a pillowcase, a bath towel, an ordinary pair of gloves, two nightshirts, his dressing gown, his foot muff, his fingerless gloves, and a cap. Also three coat hangers. Ottla has added letter paper, pens, journals, and a bar of soap. She gives Dora some dishcloths and an embroidered linen tablecloth. Oddly, Dora almost breaks into tears. In the hard city of Berlin, this linen is a luxury she has almost forgotten.

As his sister is leaving, Franz slips a doll into her luggage for Vera. In case Lolotte should decide to go off on a trip, you never know with dolls!

He mentions Ottla's visit to Max, saying, Everything she saw at our house appealed to her. He is mistaken. On reaching home, Ottla informs Franz that she is sending him a fifteen-kilo package and she has asked her mother to do the same.

"Fifteen kilos," says Franz. "That seems too much, fifteen kilos, what can possibly be in it? I don't want to live at your expense."

M ax arrives shortly after, curious to meet the mysterious Fräulein Diamant whom his friend has refused to say anything about. He is enormously impressed by her love for Franz. The two live in wonderful harmony, he feels. Kafka has never seemed so confident.

Dr. Ernst Weiss, who is as active and as nervous as ever (it is the nervousness of a lively but embittered man), comes to visit them. He wants to thank Franz in person. When the publisher Carl Seelig asked Kafka for some new stories, Franz felt that he had nothing worth submitting and instead sent three texts by Weiss, whose praises he sang, along with a list of the books written by this "difficult but extremely talented author."

Kafka likes Ernst. He examines him, standing there so solidly, and says to himself that "this man stays in good health, in very good health, only by an act of will. If he wanted, he could be as sickly as anyone."

Franz Werfel shows up one day in the early afternoon, a manuscript under his arm. Small, chubby, blond with blue eyes, he projects the confidence of a genius whose place in the firmament is assured. Dora, who is happy to meet him, greets him at the door. Kafka and Werfel shut themselves in the office. After a very long time, Werfel emerges. He is in tears and rushes off without a word of good-bye. Kafka is just as upset. He murmurs, "How can a person write so badly, so very badly . . ."

Werfel was expecting a shower of praise but met only with dismayed silence.

When he is obliged to judge a text, Kafka is incapable of uttering even the whitest lie, whatever the cost.

In early January the temperature drops to five degrees Fahrenheit. Franz becomes ill. High fever, shivering, exhausting fits of coughing morning and night, darken his mood.

He resigns himself to calling the doctor despite his terror of the doctor's fee, a sum that hovers in fiery figures above his bed. Before long, he is also having trouble with his digestion. He now keeps to his bed permanently.

When Max returns a second time to see him, he is horrified at the rapid decline in his friend's health and the stark deprivation in which he lives. Once back in Prague, he contacts Franz's uncle, Dr. Siegfried Löwy, a country doctor who practices in the Moravian town of Triesch. A bachelor with a special fondness for his young relative (Franz spent many of his vacations with him), he rushes off to visit his nephew on February 29 and persuades him to leave Berlin as soon as practicable.

"If you stay here, in such poorly heated rooms, so poorly fed, you'll never last the winter."

On March 14, 1924, Max is once again in Berlin. He is attending the premiere of *Jenůfa*, Janáček's opera, whose libretto he translated. Three days later, he brings Kafka back to Prague. Franz categorically refuses to let Dora accompany him. He wants at all costs to spare her his father's sarcasms, his contempt, his disrespect.

At the station, her face a blur of tears, the young woman clings to him, saying, "I don't want to leave you."

"You'll be joining me in a few days, as soon as my uncle has found a place for me in a sanatorium."

He kisses her again and again: "I have never wanted to live as much as I do now. With you."

He steps over the threshold of his parents' apartment. He looks like a recidivist being returned to a cell from which he will not emerge alive. He thinks he hears his jailer snicker behind his back: "The return of the prodigal son! The triumphal entry! Broke, and he hasn't got the strength to drag himself into bed! A total disaster! I warned you about what would happen. Once again, Herr Son has done exactly as he pleased, and this is what has come of it. When there are broken pots, I'm the one to pay for them."

He would prefer not to see even his mother, who timidly offers him chicken broth, pudding, and kefir with raspberry sauce. He hates to see her back bent in servitude. Only Marie Werner, the Fräulein, who is reserved, fair-minded, and silent, calms the rage in his heart a little.

As a rampart against his parents he asks Max, in a clipped, authoritarian tone he has never used before—the time is past for amiability—to visit him every day: "Come back tomorrow at the same time," he says at each visit.

Cloistered in his room, his eyes shut, he broods over his failure or, sick with grief, reviews the many faces of Dora, her gestures, her words of love. He feeds on these images. Waves of nostalgia constantly carry him back to Berlin, to his six months of freedom far from the supervision of his parents.

For the first time in his life, he had lived day after day with a woman. He opened his eyes, Dora was nearby, he closed his eyes, Dora was nearby, they lived in the same house, elbow to elbow, at the same table, they slept in the same bed, cupped against each other, he had never known such joy. He murmured in her ear: I am in the arms of an angel.

When he wrote, sinking his teeth into his desk like a dog with a bone, as he put it, showing her his fangs to make her laugh, Dora would nap in her chair in front of him, because he needed her to be present. Whereas he had never written a word in front of Ottla, Felice, Milena, or Max.

"You become someone else when you write," Dora had said.

Sometimes, she had been afraid to look at his tensed face. Your features harden, your eyes are stern, cruel, painful, I don't know how to say it . . . as though you were hunting ghosts . . . Is it a knife, a weapon, in your hand?

He had read her passages from "The Burrow," on a night when he finished a chapter all in one sitting: "I live in peace in the most secret depths of my burrow, yet somewhere the enemy is tunneling a hole that will lead him straight to me. I don't mean he has a better nose than I do, but there are relentless plunderers who rummage blindly . . . and I have so many enemies! I wouldn't want, while I was scratching at the earth in despair and fury, to feel the teeth of a pursuer sinking into my thigh."

He had raised his head.

Dora was looking at him, perplexed.

"You don't have any enemies, no one wants to harm you, my love."

He burst into laughter: "My sweet, dear girl, they're only words. Come, you're not going to take this scribbling seriously!"

Together in the preceding days they had burned page after page of his manuscripts to raise the temperature in their haybox. Was it three hundred pages, or maybe five hundred? Several times Dora had stopped him: "These manuscripts cost you so much work, over so many nights, why do you want to throw them in the fire?"

He remembers having thought of Kleist at that moment.

"Seeing the flames devour my manuscripts soothes me. The more I burn, the more I am freed of my demons, I slip between their fingers. I asked dear Max, very solemnly, as I am quite capable of doing, no? I ordered him to burn— in their entirety and without reading them—my note-books, copybooks, manuscripts, and all my letters. I know he'll respect my wish."

O n the third day after his return to Prague, there are disturbing signs: he has a monstrously sore throat. Burning sensations at the limit of what is bearable. His voice has changed, it is low and hoarse. So fast! he says.

Preserves, fruit, fruit juice, water, fruit juice, water, fruit juice, fruit, preserves, water, fruit juice, fruit, pre-serves, water, lemonade, cider, fruit, water. He can swal-low nothing else. Only in small quantities.

His uncle, Dr. Siegfried Löwy, prescribes long and painful tests, to which the patient submits with a heavy heart. Franz can learn nothing specific about his condi-tion. From the moment tuberculosis of the larynx is men-tioned, the doctors speak in a cautious, stilted manner.

"A swelling, an infiltration, nothing alarming, we still don't know anything for certain," this is what he is being told, even as he is experiencing violent pain. He weighs 108 pounds in his winter clothes.

He coughs for hours morning and night. He fills his spittoon in a minute.

"A feat worthy of the Nobel Prize, wouldn't you say?" he says to Robert Klopstock, who has just come into his room.[29]

Franz met this medical student at the sanatorium in Matliary two years earlier and has been writing him without interruption since. Robert sometimes irritates him to the point of anger. The young man, who resumed his studies after the stay in Matliary, complains about everything, is forever making reproaches, and is always defeatist. True, he lives in poverty.

Franz has sent him money, arranged for his meals at the university dining hall, found him temporary posts. He has recommended him to Max, to Ottla, to his friends, he starts to worry when he has no news from him, gives

---

29 Dr. Robert Klopstock emigrated to the United States, where he became a distinguished professor of medicine, a lung specialist. He died in New York City in 1972.

him advice when he can, but "pieces of good advice," he writes Robert, "are hung between the stars, which explains why there is so much darkness."

Robert, who is as passionate about literature as about medicine, has been keen to translate a novel by Max Brod and several of Kafka's stories into Hungarian, his native tongue, and Kafka has agreed to oversee the work. He's such an appealing young man!

In the tones of a five-star general, Robert answers: "The only feat that deserves the Nobel Prize is for you to fight and get well. You still can!"

"You forget that I'm a bad soldier, no one would take me. Twice I tried to enlist, in June 1915 and June 1916. Twice the medical board declared me unfit."

They talk about Matliary, about the inmates. Kafka thinks of his neighbor who played with the sun and mirrors like a suicide playing Russian roulette. The image of this tortured man, his mouth wide open on his ulcers and giving off a pestilential odor, still makes him nauseous.

"Will I be subjected to the same tortures?" he asks himself. "It's one thing to write, one's feet in slippers, 'Torture is very important to me, my sole occupation is to experience and inflict it,' and another to be tied to the stake. With flames licking one's feet.

"Don't you find it odd, Robert, that the god of pain was not the principal god of the early religions?"

As his friend is getting ready to leave, he grabs his hand: "Do you remember the promise you made me at the sanatorium? I insist that you renew it. Right away."

Three weeks confined to his room.

Sprawled on his sofa and looking out his open window, he sees roofers at the top of the steeple on the Russian church. They are climbing, working, singing in the wind and rain. He watches them, astonished: "What are they but prehistoric giants?"

He is no longer opposed to the sanatorium since, as he says to his uncle, "I can't oppose the fever, one hundred degrees has become my daily bread."

He is relieved to leave his parents' apartment and Prague. "One's native city," as he confided to a young friend, "is always inhospitable, a place of memories, of melancholy, of pettiness, of shame, of temptation, a place where one's resources were put to poor use."

At the sanatorium, Dora will be able to join him. Together, things will be easier.

"Let's go," he says, "the world belongs to me. *Very well.*"

Dora arrives at Wiener Wald a few hours after Franz. It is a university sanatorium, wonderfully situated, plush, oppressive.

She walks into the ward through the rows of beds, the patients with their livid complexions and hollow cheeks coughing and spitting in funereal chorus. She is looking for her Franz. She doesn't hear him calling, his voice is only a murmur. She sees him, almost faints. Gaunt face, eyes burning with fever, hands of a bird, which she kisses frantically to hide her distress.

She keeps repeating, "I'll never leave you again, dear love, I'll never leave you."

She hears him whisper in her ear, "I'm the one who will be leaving you."

Despite insistent requests from Franz Werfel and repeated entreaties from Max, the director, Professor Hajek, refuses to assign Herr Kafka a private room: "All I can see in him is the patient in bed 18."

For the fever he prescribes liquid pyramidon three times a day; for the coughing, demopon, which is ineffective, and atropine. Franz is given hard candies with analgesics, and his throat is sprayed with mentholated oil. His larynx is so swollen that when he swallows, Franz feels as if shards of glass are embedded in his throat. He can no longer eat.

Pointing to his throat, he asks the nurse, "What does it look like in there?"

She answers frankly, "A witch's cauldron."

Despite treatment, the fever never drops below 101 degrees. Professor Hajek confirms the diagnosis: tuberculosis of the larynx. And of the epiglottis.

The lungs are in such poor condition that Hajek soon refuses to keep the patient on, saying that he is beyond the help of any specialist.

"The only palliatives," he says before turning away, "would be morphine and pantopon."

The care is so hideously expensive that—for the first time—Franz asks Max to offer his most recent stories to a publisher *right away* (he double-underlines the words). "'Josephine' will have to rescue me," he writes, "there is nothing else for it."

Dora, unbeknownst to Franz, adds a few lines to the postcard: "Professor Hajek has decided that Franz's condition is very serious, we are moving to Dr. Hoffmann's sanatorium in Kierling, near Vienna."

The day before the departure, a few feet from his bed, a man is dying. The doctors had let the man wander around earlier with pneumonia and a fever of 106. Franz can hear his death rattle. His gasping is so loud that, at times, Franz must bury his head under his pillows, suffocating himself.

A priest and his helpers recite prayers at the patient's bedside, hold his hand, speak to him in a comforting voice. When he sinks into a coma, they administer the last rites. They stay with him, whereas the doctors slipped away long ago and are asleep in their beds.

The next day, Franz relates his distress only to Max: "I've already cried several times today for no reason. My neighbor died during the night."

To calm his fear, he closes his eyes, allows images to flash past. A landscape lashed by rain. A deserted road. In the distance, a car. Slowly it comes close. The beam of its headlights pierces the ground fog. It is an open-topped car. The chauffeur is wearing a mackintosh and a visored cap. Clutching the steering wheel, he peers at the road through aviator's glasses. Behind him, lying crosswise, is a young woman, her hair and clothes streaming with water, her arms outspread, one hand gripping the door handle, the other holding the driver's seat. Her face is indistinct.

The car swerves to avoid a rabbit that has leaped into the headlights. The young woman's body slumps to the left. The bridegroom is revealed. Swathed in blankets like a mummy, he is stretched out on the back seat. He is sick and, judging from his appearance, incurable.

It's a romantic movie!

He opens his eyes.

"The reality," he says, "is quite different. A scene from a comedy. Dora's knee is poking into my stomach, my feet are submerged in a pool of water, and my spittoon—it is just too funny!—has emptied onto my neck."

Early in the morning of April 20, they leave Dr. Hajek's sanatorium. An open-topped car is put at their disposal, nothing else being available.

Stormy weather threatens. They are barely on the road when a series of hailstorms sweeps through, accompanied by thunder and high winds, an incredible din, followed by brief lulls. Lying in the back of the vehicle, Kafka is perhaps thinking about Beethoven or Mahler, both of whom died while a storm raged. Probably one much like this.

During the trip, Dora stands teetering above him. He protests, "Sit down, you're going to fly away."

"Don't try to talk, dear heart, nothing will separate me from you."

During a respite, she hears Franz whisper to her, "The pneumatic tires hum on the asphalt like the projector at the cinematograph."

He is fascinated by the cinematograph. In Berlin, he recounted his favorite movies to Dora scene by scene, some of them with their dialogue: *Little Lolotte*, which made him cry, *The Catastrophe at the Dock*, which he found too sad, *The Gallant Guardsman*, *The Thirsty Gendarme*, and *Alone At Last*, which amused him enormously. *Slaves of Gold* is a film that should be memorized from start to finish, he had said.

And yet in Prague, at a time when he was out every evening, he went to the cinematograph only rarely.

"Why?" Dora asked.

"I identified too strongly with the actors. When someone suffered or died on the screen, I would see myself suffer or die. Certain images haunted me to the point of obsession, my insomnia grew worse."

He preferred documentaries. He remembers the last program he saw, one Sunday afternoon at the Lido-Bio. The first film, *Shivat Zion*, was on the work of the pioneers in Palestine, the deserts transformed into orchards, the clean new villages, the model schools and day care centers.

The next film caused waves of applause. It showed Jewish athletes, big, square-shouldered men with slender waists and gleaming muscles, exercising in the Karlsbad stadium. These demigods were training for footraces, for the high jump, the pole vault, the pommel horse, the rings, as though their parents and great-grandparents had practiced these sports all their lives. As though the Zionist utopia and the rebuilding of the body were linked.

This documentary made a durable impression on Franz, but without troubling his nights.

He confided to Dora another of his manias: in Prague, going home at night on the tram, he would lean out of the car as far as he could, within an ace of losing his balance, and, on the fly, in snatches, he would try to read every movie poster and examine every photograph. He never tired of it.

Once home again, in the bathroom, he would invent scenes from comic films for his sisters. They would laugh and beg him to continue.

All he needed was a single sentence to imagine a whole long story.

For example?

"The door opened a crack. A revolver appeared at the end of an outstretched arm."

Another?

"Two children, alone in an apartment, climb into a steamer trunk, when suddenly the lid slams shut."

"It was Sunday afternoon, and through the glass-paneled door Anna saw the landlady tuck up her skirts."

"I don't exactly understand you," Dora had said. "The posters are something you play with, you inhale, you don't want to miss one of them. But the movies you avoid, you're afraid of them?"

He laughed: "You nod your head just the way Hasidic rabbis do!"

He enters the Kierling sanatorium on Dora's arm. Thanks to recommendations from several prominent figures, he has been assigned a lovely room on the third floor with southern exposure, overlooking a garden.

The bad weather continues, low clouds, rain, cold wind, but the air is wonderful, it feels as though one is inhaling health. The food is everything that could be hoped for, and Dora is allowed to prepare meals just as she pleases. Here, as at Professor Hajek's, the rule is that Dora may spend the whole day with Franz and only has to leave him at night. She is staying at a nearby farm.

Franz Werfel, in gratitude, has sent him his latest book, *Verdi: A Novel of the Opera*,[30] and some beautiful roses. Ottla has sent peonies, his favorite flower. From the farm Dora has brought back a lilac branch whose buds have just opened. Franz is intoxicated by their scent, spring has entered his room.

He is very weak but in good hands. The treatments start to take effect. His larynx is injected once or twice a day with alcohol, an extraordinarily painful procedure. He asks Dora to leave the room while the injections are being performed, refusing to have her present while he is tortured. For several hours afterward he finds relief. He can swallow again.

Two days after their arrival, they look up to see Robert Klopstock barrel into the room.

He had announced his intention to visit Franz at Dr. Hajek's sanatorium. Franz had managed to dissuade him only with great effort. He had lectured him: "No acts of violence, Robert, no sudden trip to Vienna, you know how afraid I am of violence and yet you always start in!"

From Berlin, from Prague, from Wiener Wald, Franz has sent him health bulletins and the full details of his

---

30 The dedication reads: "To Franz Kafka, venerated poet and friend, with all my wishes for a prompt recovery, Werfel."

treatment. Robert knows exactly what is happening to the patient for whom he has decided to interrupt his medical studies. Here he comes, as tall as a tower—can he possibly have grown taller?—with his fine pink cheeks, his rumpled hair, and his big smile. His smile vanishes as he registers the changes since his last visit to Franz in Prague, which was only . . . how long ago? A few weeks?

An emaciated face and arms, a body with no thickness under the sheets, and eyes . . . eyes sunk in their sockets, which pain has filled with darkness.

Robert stutters, "You . . . whether you like it or not, I'm staying."

"You're crazy, completely crazy," Franz murmurs. "I am not Bismarck. He could have a private physician, I cannot!"

Franz is delighted. The presence of this big young man, his white blouse like a coat of armor, the strength he radiates, reassure him. Robert is a good doctor, it's agreeable to put oneself in his hands. And he will give Dora a respite, force her to go outside a little. Evenings, he'll be able to distract her, she worries so much.

He calls their trio "the little family." Robert and Dora do their utmost to provide tiny pleasures for him: at each meal, they serve him a glass of Tokaji, or a connoisseur's wine, or a tankard of beer. Also, strawberries and cherries, whose fragrance their patient inhales for a long moment before eating.

Dora manages to mix an egg or some meat broth into his purées, she doesn't rest until he has eaten everything. Preserves, fruit juices, and bottles of wine are lined up on his bedside table.

There are a few moments of gaiety.

Franz has asked his dear friend Max to send him books and journals. "The natural state of my eyes," he writes, "is to be closed, but playing with books and periodicals makes me happy."

When he was young, he drank in the catalogs of Albert Langen to the last word, then started in again at the beginning, making for inexhaustible reading. Passionate about books, he did not really want to own or read them. He wanted to see them, finger them, convince himself that they existed. He sometimes spent hours in front of the shop window at the Taubeles bookstore or at Taussig & Taussig, he never tired of it.

Max arrives at Kierling on Monday, May 12, after traveling for twenty-four hours and changing trains twice, once in Vienna and again in Klosterneuburg.

That day, the alcohol injections had wearied Franz to the point of fainting. Then his fever surged and he had endless coughing fits. Faced with Max, whose visit he had looked forward to with such joy, he lacks the strength either to smile or to hold out his hand. A few words, a barely audible murmur: "I have two saws across my throat."

Max, distraught, makes a sorry sight. Ever since Prague, the trip had unfolded under the sign of death. Dora and Robert push him into the hallway. Themselves inconsolable, they do their best to console him.

A few days later, on May 20, Franz thanks his friend for the book he has sent and begs his forgiveness for having spoiled his visit.

"Farewell, thank you for everything. Warm greetings to Felix and Oskar."

These are the last words of his last letter to Max.

When, in response to the pantopon, he sinks into slumber, dreams come to torment him, always the same ones. His father, not the aging man he is today but the giant he was in the prime of life, fills the stage. Next to him cowers his son, five or six years old, a packet of bones, frail and narrow, a stutterer in his father's presence.

The child has been awakened by a nightmare, he cries out. His mother rushes in. He complains, "I'm thirsty." She brings him a glass of water from the kitchen, kisses him: "Go back to sleep, my son." She returns to her husband's bed. The child is no longer sleepy. Partly to irritate his parents, partly to amuse himself, he starts sniffling again: "I'm still thirsty." His mother doesn't come. Stubbornly, he cries all the louder.

He wails. His father, monstrous in a floating white nightshirt, his head touching the ceiling, rises up before him: "Spoiled brat." He raises his hand.

"Don't hit me," cries the child. A hand grabs him by the scruff of the neck, drags him to the *pawlatsche*, the inner balcony, and opens the French window. The child sobs, strikes out with his arms and legs.

"You little snotnose," the father shouts, "I'll squash you flat if you keep sniveling." He shuts the window.

The boy stays out on the balcony alone, terrorized by the courtyard below him as dark as a well. He waits, his teeth chattering, for his mother to rescue him.

She doesn't come.

Now a little older, nine or ten, he is at the public swimming pool. His father has decided to teach him to swim. They are together in a dark, narrow changing cabin, the colossus fills the space, his torso, arms, and thighs are those of a gladiator. His damp armpits emit a powerful, acrid smell that turns the boy's stomach.

Naked, the two walk forward in the sun over creaking boards, one with his chest out, his head high, his legs apart, the other a small teetering stick figure whose eyes are at the level of a heavy cock, thick, tumescent, displaying a sinuous network of raised veins, blue and translucent, through which the boy can see blood pulse. Two enormous testicles, smooth as ivory balls, clap against one thigh and then the other.

Huge mitts hand him a sausage and a giant mug of beer. A thunderous voice tells him to eat it all, to drink it down to the foam.

He emerges from these dreams exhausted, glazed in sweat.

"Will my father dog me to the grave?" he asks Dora.

Since arriving at the sanatorium, he has written very few letters, he has neither the freedom nor the strength for it. Late April, a few lighthearted lines to his parents: "My treatment consists of very lovely compresses and inhalations." With their permission, he allows himself to be a lazy correspondent. He assigns Dora and Robert the task of sending his parents news of him and of talking on the telephone to his beautiful, beloved Ottla, and to Elli, Valli, Max, and his friends.

Robert continually reports on the extraordinary, the inexhaustible love of Dora for Franz. "It's an unlimited

source of good," he says. When Ottla thanks him for staying at her brother's bedside, he exclaims in his poor German: "It is true privilege! When he turn his bright eyes
full of life on us, me jolly happy, marvelous, magnificence
of God, those two, so good together!"

Ottla is the only one of the three sisters who is able
to come to Kierling. She stays just for the day. She brings
her brother the red quilt he has asked for. He spends his
whole day outside, on the veranda, and the air has grown
colder.

Julie and Hermann Kafka write or telephone almost
every day. When they announce by express letter that
they intend to visit, Franz finds the strength to answer
them immediately, so daunting is the prospect.

The letter is a long and good one. He first suggests
the joy they would find in being quietly together for a
few days in a beautiful place, a glass of beer in hand, as in
the days when his father would bring him to the public
swimming school. Then he allows that, for the moment,
he is not worth seeing: "I'm not pretty to look at." But
he is starting to get stronger thanks to Dora and Robert,
whose help it would be impossible to imagine from a distance. But, he goes on, "The shock of having tuberculosis
of the larynx has weakened me more than it should have
done, and in addition to my usual complaints I am having

stomach upsets. And I cannot speak above a whisper. Too many reasons argue against your coming."

In closing he reassures them: "The professor has noticed a big improvement, the signs are all good. Robert never leaves me for a moment, he puts all his strength into thinking about me instead of his exams."

What if the warning is not enough? And what if his mother decides to make the trip alone, as she has hinted that she might? She would collapse at the sight of her son, it would be terrible for both of them.

Robert entreats Julie Kafka: "Frau, dear frau, you possibly provoke fatal agitation in your son."

I s there a letter from Bedzin?"

Franz asks the same question every morning. The silence, growing longer daily, makes him anxious. Dora tries to reason with him: "You don't know my father. He is a completely inflexible man, he has never compromised with the Law. You introduced yourself to him not as a believer but as a penitent. And don't forget that I fled his roof. He no longer recognizes me as his daughter."

"But you are his daughter. And I have expressed my strong desire to have ancestors, a wife, descendants."

"The Baal Shem Tov has taught me that every human being is in direct contact with God. An evening doesn't pass, a morning, when I don't recite the prayer that you now know as well as I do: 'Praise unto Thee, Eternal One, our God and God of the universe, may all flow from your sacred hand.'"

The answer from Bedzin arrives. Herr Herschel Diamant, as on every occasion when he must make a decision, has consulted the rabbi he most respects, Mordechai Alter. The saintly man read Dr. Kafka's letter and pronounced a single word: "No."

Franz, his face a mask, hands the letter to Dora: "Another shipwreck. My final defeat."

"Dear Franz, I am already your wife, body and soul. We cannot be joined more closely than we already are. I have no need of my father's blessing. You are my husband before God."

Dora has said nothing about the pressure being exerted on her by Dr. Hoffmann, his wife, and the hospital personnel. Every day they harass her: "You must get married. You must conform to basic rules of morality, of propriety. We cannot tolerate your disgraceful behavior in our sanatorium!"

One morning when Franz is terribly low, Dr. Hoffmann calls Dora into his office. He introduces her to a rabbi he has summoned from Vienna, shows her the marriage forms all filled out, hands her a prayer shawl. Dora is outraged. She leaves the office in tears, slamming the door in their faces.

She knows that Franz wants to marry her so that his parents, his father especially, will accept her as a daughter-in-law.[31] And support her.

"They already love me," she says to Robert, "I'm sure of it, you've heard them on the telephone, they don't know how to thank me, how to show their gratitude."

On May 26, 1924, he writes his last letter. To his most beloved parents. Six lines. He corrects a misunderstanding: "My desire to drink water in large glasses and eat fruits is no less than my desire for beer. But for the moment I am making only slow progress."

---

31 Thanks to Max Brod, Dora received Kafka's German-language royalties as though she were his wife.

Up to his death, he believed that he made only slow progress in everything he undertook: the piano, the violin, Italian, English, Hebrew, German studies, anti-Zionism, Zionism, carpentry, gardening, literature, his attempts to marry. His teacher, Herr Beck, had been right to warn his father: "Leave him in fifth grade, too much hurry can be very costly. This is a slow child."

He tells himself, I have finished none of my novels, I have abandoned several of my stories in the middle of a word.

I am leaving behind only fragments.

I have brought none of my projects to fruition.

He thinks of "Billig," the collection of travel guides that Max and he had imagined one day when they were wandering around Montmartre with empty pockets, guidebooks that would have replaced the tiresome Baedekers and given tourists the information they really needed: the addresses of inexpensive bistros, hotels, pastry shops, clothing stores, and museums. Their first titles: "Billig Paris" (Paris on the Cheap) and "Billig Switzerland."

He remembers that he asked Max to jettison "Richard and Samuel," the novel they had started writing together, and which Max had such high hopes for.

I finish nothing, not even my sentences, which . . .

He is almost voiceless. The doctors have recommended that he temporarily stop speaking. He communicates with Dora and Robert through written notes. At first he makes a game of it, writes only part of what he wants to say, they have to guess the rest. He nods if they are right, signals with his hand if they are wrong.

He takes an interest in the flowers that fill his room.

"Look at the lilac, fresher than morning," he writes to Robert.[32]

"Show me the columbine. It is too brightly colored to be with the others."

"The hawthorn is too hidden, too much in the shadows."

"The lilac is wonderful, isn't it? It is dying, but it still drinks, it still gets drunk."

"Do you have a moment? Then please, give a little water to the peonies, they are so fragile."

"A bird has gotten into the room. That's why people like dragonflies."

Several other scraps of paper refer to food and drink.

---

32 Robert kept Kafka's "conversation slips." The ones addressed to him use the formal mode of address. Only a portion of them have been published.

"Ask if there is some good mineral water, just out of curiosity."

"A dying man doesn't drink."

"Why didn't I try the beer at the hospital? Lemonade . . . everything was so plentiful."

When he feels well, he remembers his vacations in Italy, Riva, and the Baltic. To the brief message he often adds a drawing or a map.

Others are about his parents, or about Dora and Robert.

"My father is pleased to receive an express letter, but it angers him too."

"If a man marked for death can stay alive from happiness, then I will stay alive."

"Put your hand on my forehead to give me courage."

"There are always possibilities waiting to unfold."

"Max's birthday is on May 27, don't forget."

"How long can I stand for you to stand me?"

"Where is the eternal spring? I've thought of every possible miracle, but the illusion didn't last."

His last missive, written as the doctor left his room: "That's how help always leaves, without giving any help."

The pain in his throat is unbearable. The alcohol injections are no longer having an effect. Only the morphine and the pantopon offer relief, but for shorter and
shorter periods. Robert refuses to increase the dosage for
fear that Franz's heart will give out.

Today he has stopped taking food and drink. He prefers
to die of hunger and thirst, a thirst that drives him crazy,
rather than swallow a mouthful of water that is not enough
to satisfy him and inflicts a torture worse than thirst.

Dora constantly wets his lips, gives him the scent of
his favorite fruits to inhale: strawberries, a slice of pine-
apple. She repeats under her breath like a litany: "My
love," "My sweet," "Dear heart."

She has gone up to Robert's room.
"How can you rest when he is dying of hunger,
when he's been dying of thirst for the last two days?"

She hammers at his chest with her fists: "Do something, please, please, don't abandon him, you're a doctor,
do something . . ."

She collapses onto Robert's shoulder, her nerves
relax, she sobs quietly, then more and more violently, as

though venting waves of indignation, of incomprehension: "Where is the God of justice? Where is the God of compassion?"

Too moved to speak—and what would he say?—Robert wraps his arms around her, strokes her hair until, exhausted, she grows quiet. He hands her a glass of water in which he has dissolved a sleeping draft: "Rest here for a while. I'll go downstairs and be with him."

The morphine notwithstanding, Franz has eaten nothing for three days. He has drunk a little water. At this point he receives the proofs for A Hunger Artist, a collection that includes the title story and three others, "First Sorrow," "A Little Woman," and "Josephine the Singer."

He has been expecting the proofs impatiently: "They waited until now to send me the material!"

He immediately starts reading the texts, pencil in hand. He works his way through them intently, seemingly not unhappy with his writing. He finishes one set of proofs. He starts in on the second. Robert watches him out of the corner of his eye, while pretending to read a medical journal. He sees the pencil and the proofs fall to the ground. He goes to pick them up, stops.

Kafka is crying.

He is in no condition to go on correcting. He is in no condition to read the story, written two years earlier: a young man, locked in a cage, fasts before a large and enthusiastic crowd, which grows sparser with the passing days. An artist, he is obliged to fast, he can do nothing else, he fasts for forty days straight and dies to general indifference. A janitor finally sweeps the cage clean of the vermin's body mixed with dirty straw. Its place is taken by a splendid young panther, fed at regular intervals. Spectators now crowd around the cage, unwilling to move on.

The Last Day: June 3, 1924

A noise? A silence? Something must have awakened her. Leaning toward him, she listens to him breathe. Are his breaths too short? Irregular? She is afraid to turn on the light, he sleeps so shallowly. He went to sleep around midnight, relaxed, calm. Despite the pressure from Robert—"Go get some sleep, you need it, you'll be exhausted"—she has once again spent the night in his room. Chained to the bedside of a skeleton. The hands resting on the red quilt are no more than talons, and the bones show through the skin of the mummy's face.

She is afraid of dozing off. She goes out on the veranda, whose door is always slightly ajar. The night is warm. Scents rise from the surrounding gardens. A breath of air occasionally comes to her from the fields. She has looked out at this swath of countryside so many times that she can almost see it in the darkness, the cluster of tamaracks here, the houses and the steeple there, the sandy track. Her senses sharpened, she goes back inside to sit at the head of the bed.

Toward four a.m., a shrill whistle pierces her. She leaps to the telephone. Robert comes running. He immediately awakens the doctor on duty.

Two years before, Kafka had written in his *Diaries:* "There is without question something agreeable in being able to write calmly: Suffocation is a thing of inconceivable horror."

The inconceivable horror, suffocation, is happening. Air is no longer entering his lungs, despite the pneumothorax. Stretched rigid on the bed, from which he has violently thrown back the covers, his mouth wide open, no cry emerging from it, no sound, his eyes wild, bulging, Kafka begs for a breath of air, his emaciated arms extended toward the doctor. Dora, her hands pressed to her mouth, moans as though from stomach cramps. She steps forward, falls at the foot of the bed, faints.

A little before noon, Robert asks her to post an express letter to Franz's parents. She limply refuses: "I don't want to leave him."

Robert insists. Tired of arguing, tired of hoping for a miracle, she obeys. A relief. She can't bear to be a helpless witness to this martyrdom, she can't bear to see this horribly emaciated body. The only part of him still living is his eyes. Eyes that implore her to put an end to his suffering.

Robert Klopstock is the only witness to this inconceivable horror. Suffocation. He sees his friend, with a brusque gesture, ask the nurse to leave the room. He sees him rip out his breathing tube and throw it against the wall with surprising force.

He sees him suffocate, he sees the throat distend, offer itself to be sacrificed. He hears his friend pant, he hears him say: "You have always promised me that you would. You are torturing me, you have always tortured me, and you continue to! I will die all the same!"

Robert feels his legs go weak. He tells himself, I am twenty-five years old, I am a doctor, how can I kill the man that I admire most in all the world? That I love like a father, a teacher who has given me, taught me so much?

But can I just allow the excruciating pain of his death agony to go on indefinitely?"

He prepares a syringe.

"More, more, isn't it obvious that your dosages have no effect?"

Robert doesn't answer, he is silently crying. Suddenly he hears Franz cry out: "Kill me, or else you're a murderer!"

Now he is hallucinating. He calls to his sister: "Elli, don't come so close. There, yes, that's better."

Robert doesn't turn away. He sees the face relax, the body grow calm, slide into the silence of the shadows.

Dora comes back from the post office with a bunch of flowers. She leans toward her fiancé's face, kisses him on the cheek.

"Do you want to smell the roses, my Franz, their delicious scent?"

She thinks she hears him breathe. She thinks she sees the left eye open. She gently hugs the man she loved so much.

She no longer hears his heart beat.

Franz Kafka has escaped.

Franz Kafka was buried at Prague's New Jewish Cemetery on June 11, 1924, at four o'clock in the afternoon. The day was cold, the sky was growing dark as a procession of about a hundred people gathered around the grave, the women in black veils, the men in top hats. While the rabbis intoned the kaddish and the coffin was lowered, Dora cried out, slipping from Max's supporting grip, and fainted.

Hermann Kafka disliked displays of this sort. He turned away from Dora lying on the ground and walked

to the edge of the grave. He was the first to throw a handful of powdery, pebble-filled soil onto his son's casket. He
avoided looking at his daughter Ottla, stiff, silent, her
eyes as blank as a ghost's.

M ax Brod claimed that on the way back, as he was
passing the town hall, he had noticed that the clock
had stopped: the hands pointed to four o'clock exactly.

E ight days later at 11:00 in the morning on June 19,
1924, at a memorial service held in a small theater and
attended by more than five hundred people, Max Brod
and a number of other writers spoke and offered eulogies.

An actor, Hans Hemuth Koch, read two of Kafka's
texts. The first, "A Dream," begins: "Joseph K. was dreaming. It was a beautiful day, and he was going for a walk.
But hardly had he set out when he found himself in the
cemetery."

The second, "An Old Parchment," ends with these
words: "Workers and peasants! The safety of the nation
lies in our hands. But the task is beyond our powers. We
have in fact never claimed to be capable of such a task. It
is a misunderstanding, and it is causing our death."

After 1924

HERMANN AND JULIE KAFKA

Hermann Kafka died in 1931, and his wife, Julie, in 1934. Both lie buried beside their son. The names of all three and some verses in Hebrew are carved on the modest obelisk marking their grave.

ELLI, VALLI, AND OTTLA

Elli, her husband, Karl Hermann, and their three children, Felix, Gerti, and Hanne; and Valli, her husband, Josef Pollak, and their daughter Lotte were all deported to Lodz in Poland, where they were killed in 1944 during the liquidation of the ghetto.

Ottla convinced her husband, Joseph David, who was classified as an Aryan, to divorce her in order to save their two daughters, Vera and Helen Davidova. Shortly after, Ottla registered herself as a Jew. In August 1942 she was arrested and sent to the Theresienstadt concentration camp near Prague. The following year, she volunteered to escort a convoy of 1,260 orphans that she understood was traveling to Denmark. On arriving at Auschwitz on October 7, they were all sent directly to the gas chambers. Ottla Kafka's name is the sixth on the list of that day's victims.

A plaque resting against the headstone of the family grave commemorates Elli, Valli, and Ottla, all three of whom died at the hands of the Nazis.

Of Kafka's seven nieces and nephews, only three survived: Vera, Helen, and Marianne.

Marianne, Valli's eldest daughter, married a man named George Steiner and fled to London. By an extraordinary coincidence, Marianne encountered Dora in a London real estate office and recognized her. Learning that Dora was in terrible financial straits, Marianne offered her the English-language royalties of her uncle's works.

In 1931 the German parliament seated 107 members of the Nazi Party, and Felice fled Berlin for Switzerland with her husband and two children. In her suitcase she packed the hundreds of letters and telegrams Franz had sent her. Few are missing. The letters are so numerous that they might fill a suitcase all to themselves. Does she, in Geneva, reread a few of them on nostalgic evenings? Or does she tell herself that the past is past, leave it be?

By 1936, the position of Jews in Europe seemed so precarious that Felice emigrated to the United States. Before embarking, she rented a safe-deposit box for her papers. As a businesswoman, she could not fail to know that they constituted a valuable property. She hadn't forgotten that Max Brod saved the smallest scrap written by Franz as a relic. To her own letters she added those given to her by Grete Bloch on her way through Geneva.

The letters lay undisturbed in the safe-deposit box for nearly twenty years. In 1955, Felice sold the rights to Schocken Books of New York. They would be published only in 1967, seven years after her death and forty-three after Kafka's. Like all German Jews, Felice knew the publisher Salman Schocken, a wealthy philanthropist who had created the publishing house Schocken Verlag in Berlin. When Hitler passed a decree in 1933 that

Jewish writers could be published only by Jewish publishers, Max Brod immediately contacted Salman Schocken to persuade him to buy the rights to Kafka's books from the non-Jewish publishers who were no longer allowed to sell them. As an inducement, Max offered him global rights to Kafka's published works, as well as to any posthumous works. Felice therefore had no choice but to turn to Schocken.

A brief word about this unusual man. Expelled by Hitler, Salman Schocken emigrated first to Palestine, where he founded a new publishing company and bought the newspaper *Ha'aretz*. In 1940 he moved to the United States, a country better suited to his ambitions, and left Schocken House in the hands of his son, Gustav. Strong in his faith, Salman created Schocken Books as soon as he arrived in New York. His first collaborator was Hannah Arendt, a German immigrant.[33]

Bought in 1980 by Random House, Schocken Books is today a division of Bertelsmann, a German consortium!

It was most likely to Erich Heller and Jürgen Born, who edited the book, that Felice offered her letters and

---

33 When a journalist asked her toward the end of her life what book she would take to a desert island, Hannah Arendt answered, "My American passport."

those of Grete's in her possession. The scene can be imagined: an elderly but still sprightly lady introduces herself to the two men and unpacks before their astonished, their dazzled, their incredulous eyes the confessions and most intimate secrets of the author of "The Metamorphosis." We can guess the emotions that coursed through them, the feverish nights they spent deciphering the letters, putting them in order. Day after day, they witnessed his descent into hell, his torments, his devouring passion. Writing to have the right to live.

By 1955, Kafka had been translated into almost every language and honored in almost every nation. They could guess the extreme interest this discovery would arouse. Did they consult Max Brod in Tel Aviv, who still had his friend's manuscripts and letters?

Where are the letters that Felice wrote to Franz a century ago? Were they burned? By Franz, as he suggests in a letter to Robert Klopstock? Might there be a few of them in Israel in the files of Max Brod?

GRETE BLOCH

She had neither Felice's foresight nor her luck. Against the advice of her friends, she fled to Italy, where she was arrested and most likely deported. She had entrusted the second half of her letters from Kafka to an attorney in

Florence. At the end of the war, this attorney gave them to Max Brod, who sent them to Schocken Books in New York. The entire batch, some seventy letters in all, was then published. None of those that Grete sent to Franz has survived—the letters he refused to give back.

JULIE WOHRYZEK

Of the letters that Franz Kafka sent to Julie, probably quite small in number, none are known to exist. And nothing is known of Julie in the years that followed her engagement to Franz, beyond her death in a psychiatric institution.

MILENA JESENSKÁ

In 1924, the year of Kafka's death, Milena obtained a divorce from her husband and took up with an Austrian count, a Communist. In 1927 she married a talented architect, Jaromir Krejcar, with whom she had a daughter, Honza. After contracting septicemia during her pregnancy, Milena suffered such unbearable pain that she turned to morphine for relief and had difficulty weaning herself from it.

In 1936, separated from her husband, she devoted herself to politics. A Communist, she was excluded from the party for having denounced the Stalinist purges.

When Hitler invaded Czechoslovakia, Milena—though a non-Jew—wore the yellow star in the streets of Prague. Was it her relationship with Kafka that she was acknowledging publicly with this yellow star sewn to her collar?

Active in the Resistance, she was arrested by the Gestapo in 1940 and sent to Ravensbrück, where she died on May 17, 1944. At this concentration camp, she told the story of her life and loves to Margarete Buber-Neumann, who, once freed, wrote a biography of the liberated and radiant woman she so admired, *Milena*. The name is forever linked to Kafka's.

The *Letters to Milena* were the first to be published, well before the *Letters to Felice*. Milena had put them in the hands of the editor Willy Haas, the husband of her close friend, Jarmila. The incomplete 1951 edition was corrected in 1981. The definitive edition appeared in 1983.

When Kafka died, Milena wrote an obituary published in the Prague newspaper *Narodni listy*:

The day before yesterday, June 3, 1924, Dr. Franz Kafka, a German writer from Prague, died at the Kierling sanatorium near Vienna. Few people here knew him because, fearful of the world, he kept to his own path. His illness gave him an almost miraculous

*sensitivity and an intellectual refinement that allowed
no compromises, however terrifying the consequences.
He was shy, anxious, gentle, and kind, but his books—
the most important in all of young German literature—
were cruel and painful. He saw the world as filled with
invisible demons that destroy a defenseless man. He
was too lucid and too wise to live, too weak to fight.
He was of those who know that they are powerless,
who submit, and in so doing cover the victor with
shame. His books, filled with dry-eyed irony, describe
the horror of being misunderstood, of innocent blame.
He was an artist who kept his hearing, when the deaf
thought they were safe.*

DORA DIAMANT OR DYMANT

Her life reflects the historical upheavals of her time and,
more specifically, the trials of Communists and Jewish
Communists, who were victims of Hitler's and Stalin's
persecutions.

After a short stay in Poland, Dora returned to Berlin,
where she studied theater. In 1929 she joined the Communist Party and met a Marxist economist, Lutz Lask,
whom she married in 1932. Shortly after the birth of
her daughter, Marianne, Lask was arrested by the Gestapo. He escaped and fled to Moscow, where Dora and

Marianne joined him. He was imprisoned by Stalin in a Siberian gulag, returning twenty years later a broken man, almost blind, but still a Marxist! He owed his release to the extraordinary tenacity of his mother, who for over twenty years wrote petitions to every department of Soviet authority and to the president of East Germany.

Separated from her husband, whom she was never to see again, Dora lived first in Sebastopol, then in Yalta. In 1938 she managed to cross into Switzerland with her daughter and then to reach The Hague and finally England. Classified as an enemy alien, she was detained on the Isle of Man. She was freed in 1942 and moved to London, where she worked as a seamstress, a cook, and a theater critic.

At the invitation of the Tel Aviv city council, Dora traveled to Israel in 1950. She stayed there for four months, thanks to Kafka's English royalties. She renewed her acquaintance with Max Brod, once again regretting that, despite his insistent entreaties, she had not given him the trove of Franz's manuscripts and letters. She had obstinately refused, faithful to the promise she had made her fiancé to burn his writings.

In Israel she discovered that the new immigrants, having escaped from hell, read Kafka differently from Europeans. They found comfort in his writings, took courage from his work, which they understood immediately and unreservedly. Dora spent several weeks at the Kibbutz En Sharod, where she inquired into the rules and ideals of the pioneers. She told them about Kafka and the dream that haunted him of an ideal community, whose laws he had set down as a jurist and an ascetic in a very brief text, "The Community of Non-owning Workers." It was written in 1919, though at whose request is unknown. Women are excluded from this community, its members are forbidden to possess or accept money, and each must earn his keep solely by his work. Lawyers are barred from membership.

On the trip home, she stopped in Paris, where she met the French actor and director Jean-Louis Barrault. He was directing a production of *The Trial* in an adaptation by André Gide. At that time she also met Marthe Rob-ert, who was engaged in translating Kafka's *Diaries* into French. A lively friendship developed between the two women. Marthe Robert traveled to London several times to hear Dora talk about Kafka.

Haunted by her memories, Dora transcribed them as they flooded back to her. These were gathered as *Notes inédites de Dora Dymant sur Kafka* and published in France in 1952 by Éditions Évidences.

Dora died at the age of fifty-three in total poverty. She was buried in London on August 15, 1952, and Marthe

Robert was one of the few people present. Today, her headstone carries these words of Robert Klopstock's: "Who knows Dora, knows what love means."

The thirty-five letters from Franz, her "treasure," along with twenty notebooks and a large stack of loose pages, were confiscated from her by the Gestapo during a search of her apartment. Dora never forgave herself for not saving these materials by entrusting them to Max.

To this day, no portion of these texts has resurfaced, despite extensive research.

What remains are Dora's letters to Max Brod and to Marthe Robert. But none of those written to Franz.

ERNST WEISS

A surgeon and a talented writer, Weiss emigrated to France in early 1933. On the day Hitler entered Paris, he shot himself in the head.

FRANZ WERFEL

He became the fourth husband of Alma Mahler (who, after the composer's death, married Oskar Kokoschka, then Walter Gropius). A successful author, Werfel managed to leave occupied Paris and reach the United States in the company of a large number of artists and writers. He settled in California, where movie adaptations of his

Song of Bernadette and *Jacobowsky and the Colonel* made him famous. He died, just after Germany's surrender, on August 25, 1945, at the age of fifty-six. Alma's friends, including Otto Klemperer, Igor Stravinsky, Otto Preminger, Bruno Walter, and Thomas Mann's sons, attended his funeral, while Alma remained confined at home.

MAX BROD

He left Prague on March 14, 1939, with his wife, Elsa. His train left five minutes before Nazi troops closed the Czech border. A Zionist since his youth, he declined a professorship at an American university—an offer made to him thanks to Thomas Mann. Instead, he went to Palestine, his luggage containing the manuscripts, letters, and notebooks, the thirteen blue exercise books, the drawings and scribbles that he had recovered from Franz's desk at the request of Hermann and Julie Kafka and kept at his home ever since.

Once in Tel Aviv, the prolific Max Brod (eighty-three publications) became the dramaturge for the famous Habima Theater, which was founded in Moscow in 1918 to preserve Hebrew language and culture.

Until his death on December 20, 1968, Max devoted his energies to sorting the chapters, texts, and notes that Kafka had jumbled together in a sort of Chinese puzzle, starting his notebooks at both ends.

It was thanks to Max that *The Trial* was published in 1925, *The Castle* in 1926, and *Amerika* in 1927, all republished in the mid-1930s by Salman Schocken. In 1937 Max issued his biography of his friend, *Franz Kafka,* the only one of his books still in print. Like a satellite, it continues to orbit around "the one who forged the path," the destinies of the two men forever linked.

In 1948—by then Kafka had been translated into Hebrew—Max received one of the highest literary awards in Israel, the Bialik Prize.

A premonitory shadow, a forerunner of coming storms: when Max asked Schocken to return the manuscripts of Kafka's three posthumous novels, the publisher refused and, to protect them from the violence in the Middle East, locked them away in a Swiss safe-deposit box. The two men had a falling out.

In 1960 a new figure entered the scene, an English baron, born a great distance from Prague or Tel Aviv in the Indian city of Rajkot. This was Sir Malcom Pasley, a professor of German literature at Oxford. While teaching a course on Kafka—whom he loved, as he put it, like a younger brother—he was approached by one of his students, Michael Steiner, who told him that he was Kafka's grand-nephew, and that his mother, Marianne, lived in London. There she had met and befriended Edwin and

Willa Muir, her uncle's English-language translators. Pasley, as it happened, was convinced that Brod's editorial hand had distorted Kafka's work. He secured permission in 1961 from the author's heirs—Marianne, Vera, and Helen—to bring back to England in the trunk of his car two-thirds of the manuscripts deposited in Switzerland, including the thirteen notebooks of the *Diaries*. The experience was so traumatizing that Pasley felt the hairs on his head stand straight up throughout the trip. He consigned his treasure to the Bodleian Library at Oxford, where the manuscripts are preserved to this day. Assisted by eminent specialists, Jürgen Born among them, Pasley restored the original texts and their idiosyncratic punctuation. The English edition of the *Diaries* is to this day more complete than the German.

Max Brod watched these developments with growing irritation. Critics were attacking him more and more vocally: he had not executed his friend's will and burned the manuscripts, he had made cuts, changed the order of the chapters, and even invented certain passages. Reproaches were accumulating.

Max, who was childless, left the Kafka texts in his possession, *The Trial* in particular, to his secretary and mistress, Esther Hoffe. In 1988 Esther sold this manuscript to the German Literature Archive in Marbach,

Germany, at an auction organized by Sotheby's for $1.9 million. Hoffe had previously sold twenty-two letters and ten postcards that Kafka had written to Brod at private sales in Germany.

When Esther Hoffe died in 2007 at the age of one hundred, she bequeathed her "possessions" to her daughters, Eva and Ruth.

Israel contested the will and brought a suit against Hoffe's daughters.

So began Kafka's last trial.

Like Joseph K.'s trial, it has mobilized the efforts of dozens of lawyers.

Eva, single and in her seventies, still lives in Tel Aviv in her mother's modest apartment at 23 Spinoza Street. From the moment the trial started, Eva was besieged around the clock by journalists from all over the world. In her dark two-room apartment, stacks of papers rise toward the ceiling and a hundred cats purr and prowl among Kafka's manuscripts, as though sensing that the man who blackened these pages disliked their cold eyes and burning claws. The pets give off a stench that travels to the end of the street and regularly provokes complaints from the neighbors and visits from the police.

To none of the journalists who have staked out her front door, fingers on the bell, has Eva opened the door.

One of them, Elif Batuman, in an article published in the *New York Times* in September 2010, compared Eva to the doorkeeper who guards the entrance to the Law (*The Trial*, Chapter IX), a doorkeeper who, over the course of days, months, and years, allows no one to enter.

Eva and Ruth, like K., lost their case. Kafka's papers, which lay dormant in Zurich and Tel Aviv, now belong to the Israeli state. In July 2010, the ten safe-deposit boxes were emptied. What was found in them? The mystery has not been dispelled, as Eva and Ruth, despite their advanced age, brought an appeal. The judgment has been stayed, and no information has filtered out. Another lawsuit is in preparation. The suspense continues. How could this come as a surprise?

Author's Note

I remember that during the first year I lived in Copenhagen, in a big house by a lake where Frederiksborg Castle was reflected with its green copper roof and its eight towers, I listened from morning till night and without tiring to Mahler's Fourth Symphony, the only long-playing record I owned. My ear for music is not particularly good, in fact far from it. Years have gone by—I don't want to count how many—but I still recognize Mahler from the piece's opening strains. In order to absorb a work, I have to spend a long time with it.

I have been listening to Franz Kafka for aeons. His *Letter to His Father* is a book I have read and offered as a gift many times. Twice I have seen it performed on the stage. The second time, only a few weeks ago, the actor had a paunch and a provincial accent. He spoke in such a listless, drawling monotone that I got a headache and left.

Kafka, who dreamed of being an actor, read his own texts with forceful passion, and his friends' responses were wildly enthusiastic.

More has been written and continues to be written about Kafka than about any other writer—the interest elicited by the man and his work has not diminished over time. Yet, despite the public's great appetite for works about the author of "The Metamorphosis," *The Castle*, and *The Trial*, his own writings are no longer very widely read. *The Castle* makes us anxious, *The Trial* brings back unpleasant memories, and "The Metamorphosis," which made his friends laugh, provokes our tears.

Why have I written another book about this writer? And how did the idea come to me?

In his *Kafka*, Pietro Citati tells, very briefly, a marvelous anecdote that I had never heard before. Kafka, walking in a park in Berlin, encounters a little girl in tears; she has lost her doll. For days I pondered this meeting, the twenty or so letters that he wrote as coming from the doll. What did he tell this child to console her? I spent an inordinate amount of time composing a children's story, "Kafka and the Doll." And I wondered, Who is this Dora who records the event? At the time, I knew of only one woman in Kafka's life, Milena.

A friend gave me the collected works of Kafka, four fat volumes on Bible paper in the Pléiade edition, published with extensive notes and commentary. I concentrated on the *Diaries* and the correspondence, taking pleasure in comparing the letters written on the same day to Felice, to Max, to Ottla, savoring the differences in tone: plaintive when he addresses his first fiancée; warm and playful when he answers his sister; firm, precise, ironic, affectionate when he asks his friend for a favor. If he recounts his "night of mice" to several people, for instance, he turns it into an exercise in style, introducing variations in the story and the rhythm, taking a voluptuous pleasure in fixing life's moments, these images on the film-roll of memory, in a way that we feel. Physically.

His correspondence, richer even and more regular than his diaries, lays out Franz's daily life for us (yes, I call him by his first name). The hours, days, and years run past, a river that takes its time, meanders, widens, strays, dries up, and suddenly accelerates to the speed of a scherzo.

Here is the street along which he strides briskly, a straw boater on his head, here is Chotek Park, where he reads Kleist or Strindberg in the shade of an old tree, and here is his Hebrew teacher coming to meet him, bent under the weight of a photographic enlarger. And at nightfall, Franz pushes through the door of the Yiddish theater, where he is the first to applaud his friend Yitzhak Löwy. He casts his eyes over the audience, sets down a few lines in the notebook he always carries: "Shoulders that want to emerge from a sleeved dress" and "A face sprinkled with ashes."

Now at his office, the insurance company where he is kept so busy, he complains with a humor that predates Chaplin "of all the young women in porcelain factories constantly launching themselves into the stairway carrying great heaps of crockery." One night, I saw him cry at the movies, join a group of friends at the Café Arco, dine in disgruntlement at his parents' table, brush his hair at great length one boring Sunday. I followed him on each of his trips. The roofs in certain neighborhoods of Paris appear to me not as they are today but as I saw them when I read his "Travel Diaries."

We have none of the letters that Felice, Julie, Milena, or Dora wrote to the man who loved and pursued them as few women have been loved and pursued. We have not a line that they wrote, with the exception of eight of Milena's letters to Max. But Franz captures their image with such intensity—their tenderness, their irritation, their need, and their fear—that they enter the film he projects for us, become its stars. We follow their surges toward him and their backing away, we envy the passion they provoke, we empathize and are impatient with them—but what would I have done in their place, faced with a man who goes crazy when he is kept from writing?

From my prolonged study of his correspondence, the cardiogram of a breaking heart, I came to believe that the woman he loved most, or best, was neither Milena, nor Dora, but his youngest sister, Ottla. When his tuberculosis is diagnosed, is it not to her that he runs for shelter, to her farm in Zürau, where he spends the most peaceful eight months of his life? Is it not to her that he writes: "I never feel so well as when I am with you"?

How did you go about your work? my translator has asked me.

I started by writing a play, imagining each scene, the movements and dialogue, the location and lighting—film has accustomed us to such techniques. But it was always Kafka who held center stage; he alone spoke, he alone elicited the replies of Felice, of Julie, of Milena, of Dora, and of dear Max, the confidant of classical theater. I never made the sacrilege of putting words in Franz's mouth that he hadn't actually written. But I tinkered with the dates, the locations, and the speakers.

Once the play was finished, I was at a loss. Dissatisfied. I quickly realized that I had gone in the wrong direction. And I started all over again, both with my reading and my writing, taking exactly the same subject, Franz's singular loves, from the evening of his meeting Felice until his death.

Without realizing it, I tried to make the characters come alive and enter into dialogue, drawing farther and farther away from traditional biography. I wanted to see Franz, wanted to hear him as I had seen and heard him through all his letters: alert, anxious, thoughtful, generous, insufferable, demanding, jealous, insomniac, guilty about feeling guilt, and dependent but with a great longing for independence and freedom. And happy to be, as Franz says somewhere, "only literature."

No, I didn't write a classic biography, and I forgot to ask myself along the way what genre my writing fell into.

Fiction or nonfiction? Moments of life, perhaps? Snapshots taken on the fly? With hardly any retouching?

I finished *Kafka in Love* more than a year ago, but I continue to spend time with the Kafka family, so much does it resemble my own. We didn't live in Prague, a city

I have never visited, but in a small town in Tunisia. My mother is Hermann Kafka, but in a more exaggerated form, and my father is Julie, but fainter. He passed on to me only his fear of my mother, and he allowed her to tyrannize us in peace. We, too, went to synagogue only on the night of Yom Kippur, and our apartment, which was small and crowded, was even noisier than the Kafkas'. Like Franz, I stopped feeling ashamed of my body once I started going to the swimming pool, and I have been known to savor the sweetness of being ill. Yet I am a long way from having deciphered the body of his work, an enigma for centuries to come.